ADVERSARIES

THE LOST SOULS MC

T.L HODEL

For my work wives Becky and Dylan, who help keep me sane, and to Anthony who reminds me that sanity is sometimes overrated.

Author warning: This book contains scenes with violence, profanity, references to abuse, past trauma, PTSD triggers, suicidal thoughts and tendencies, and dubious consensual sexual scenes. If you are sensitive to such material this might not be the book for you.

<u>***Playlist***</u>

"Gangsta's Paradise" By Coolio
"Interstate Love Song" By Stone Temple Pilots
"Highway To Hell" By ACDC
"Smoke On The Water" By Deep Purple
"Winds Of Change" By Scorpions
"Old School" By Hedley
"Human" By Rag 'n' Bone Man
"Pour Some Sugar On Me" By Def Leppard
"If Today Was Your Last Day" By Nickelback
"You Give Love A Bad Name" By Bon Jovi
"Fame" By Naturi Naughton
"Move Bitch" By Ludacris
"Me Too" By Meghan Trainor
"Glamorous" By Fergie
"Dangerous Woman" By Ariana Grande
"Hells Bells" By ACDC
"I Am A Good Girl" By Christina Aguilera
"S&M" By Rihanna
"I'm A Bitch" By Meredith Brooks
"Fade To Black" By Metallica
"Sweet Child O' Mine" By Guns N' Roses

Prologue

CHASE

One year ago.

"Riley, have you seen the—" I stopped dead in my tracks.

Whatever I was going to say didn't matter because there was a goddess in my shop. A golden-haired, green-eyed goddess. Was she here for a tattoo? I sure fucking hoped so. Hell, I'd happily do one of those stupid butterflies or flowers all chicks asked for. Anything she wanted, so long as I got to mark her perfect skin.

"Seen what?" Riley's voice rang out from somewhere in the back of my head, but I had no idea what she was saying?

Whoever this girl was, she had me stunned by her beauty. I couldn't stop staring. Her red dress hugged her curves while highlighting other assets like her mouth. Full, pouty lips painted the same color. My gaze trickled down to her full breasts, pushed up and proudly on display. I had never wanted to fondle a pair of tits so much in my life.

I could practically feel them warming my palms. Bet they'd be the sweetest tits I ever sucked on. My chin tipped down to her long shapely legs.

Not as sweet as what I'd find between those thighs.

Fuck, I came out here for something. What the fuck was it?

My heart flipped when the blonde noticed me. I was transfixed, watching her eyes shimmer like polished emeralds as she took me in. That right there was the kind of woman that turned brother against brother and brought down nations. Hell, I'd kill a motherfucker just to see her on her knees.

"Hello," Riley called out, snapping her fingers.

Pay attention fuckwitt.

I cleared my throat and answered Riley, "Have you seen my coils?"

This girl was probably close to Riley's age. I should not be gawking at her like some sleazeball. Then again, she was the one that waltzed in here, looking like that.

Fuck, I really needed to stop gawking at this teenage girl and get back to work. What if she wasn't a teenager? She could be in her early twenties– then it would be okay that my dick was jumping for joy. Not that that particularly mattered.

I woke up next to an eighteen-year-old last week—still a teenager, but also an adult. No matter how drunk I got, I never crossed that threshold.

"They're in the back," Riley threw her thumb over her shoulder, "in the supply closet."

Right the coils. I really should go get those. Or...

I once again slid my gaze over the blonde's hard body.

She curled her lip back at me. "Can I help you?"

Yeah, honey, you can fucking help me.

"Sorry," I grimaced and gave my head a shake. "Don't get many girls like you in here."

And if I did, they sure as hell wouldn't still have that dress on. Girl was lucky Riley was here. My niece thought I was an upstanding guy, and I preferred to keep it that way.

"That's because it stinks of sweat," she sneered and shrugged off a shutter. "I feel dirty just being in here."

I see. So the chick was a bitch. Made sense, I guess. Based on the jewels in her ears, I assumed she had money. Wouldn't be the first stuck-up princess I reigned in.

"Not much for manners, are you?" I said, crossing my arms.

Entitled princess lifted her chin as if she was daring me to challenge her. "Not when it comes to docksider trash."

Scratch that, chick was a cunt.

"Watch it, Princess," I warned while reminding myself that Riley was right there. "I don't put up with mouthy bitches."

"What did you call me?" She snarled as if no one had ever called her a bitch to her face before. Which I found really fucking hard to believe. "Listen to me, you little insignificant piece of trash..."

Her heels clicked on the floor as she sauntered over to wave her hand in my face and fuck me if she didn't smell as good as she looked. If her voice wasn't starting to grate on my nerves, I might've found an inventive way to shut her up.

It'd been a while since I'd had a good hate-fuck. At least I think it had? Most nights were spent lost in a bottle. It was the only way I could get some peace. Who the fuck knew what I did to the random chicks I woke up beside?

My eyes narrowed on the cunt's flapping lips. She was still spewing out bullshit. I tipped my head and eyed the stuck-up way she lifted her chin. She seemed kind of familiar. Did I know her? Oh shit, I did. She was the idiot mayor's daughter. Nikki or something? What the fuck was her name?

"Scum like you aren't fit to lick the dirt off my shoes."

Cunt. That's what her name was.

I arched a brow down at the finger she was jabbing into my chest. Has no one bothered to teach this bitch a lesson?

"I eat men like you for breakfast."

Uh-huh, we'll see about that, Princess.

Enough was enough. My arm shot out, fingers wrapping around the back of her neck as I folded her over the counter and smacked my hand on her ass. The loud crack vibrating through the room was almost as satisfying as her squeal.

"What the hell do you think you're doing?!"

"What your daddy should've done," I grunted and delivered another swat, this time flicking my wrist to add a little extra oomph.

She yelped and lifted up onto her tip-toes. "You can't do this to me!"

The hell, I can't.

Watching her struggle had me tempted to punish her in another way. Anal wasn't necessarily my thing, but Goddamn, that was one fuckable ass. I hit her again, this time to see her wiggle.

Then again to hear her squeak, and again, because... fuck it, who cared why? My dick sure didn't. It throbbed with every strike I delivered and twitched along with her hips. I'd never been more turned on in my life.

Might've considered shoving my fingers in her cunt, until I noticed Riley staring at me. And not just her. That stupid jackass Mason Kessler had the dumbest smile on his face. Prick knew exactly what I was thinking. Not that I gave a shit what he thought. Riley, on the other hand...

One look at the shock twinkling in my niece's dark blue eyes, and I took a step back.

What the fuck was I thinking?

Not sure why, but I thought that would be the end of it. Nikki, however was not letting that shit go. She shot up the second I released her and took a swing at me. Smug little bitch wasn't fast enough to catch me off guard. I grabbed her wrist before she could make contact.

A chick with attitude was okay. Hell, the feisty ones were fun to fuck with. But this bitch was challenging me in my parlor. That I wouldn't tolerate. She wanted to be a bitch, fine. I'd shove that shit right back down her throat.

"The next time you come in my shop running your mouth," I bent down, getting right in her face so she'd see how serious I was, "you'll get my belt."

I could feel Riley watching me. But I was so far past giving a shit.

Nikki's eyes narrowed as she tore her arm out of my grip. "When my father hears about this—"

"You're running your mouth again." My brow arched, silently daring her to give me a reason.

One twitch, word, hell even a snide look would do. That's all I needed to take this shit to the next level. She stomped her foot, pursing her lips together, and I had to hold back the smirk threatening to break out. For half a second, I thought my wish might be granted.

Instead, Nikki flipped her hair over her shoulder and spun for the door. "Screw this; I'm calling an Uber."

"That's right, Princess," I called out while sauntering back to my office, "go running back home to daddy."

Prissy little bitch better hope I never see her again.

Chapter 1

CHASE

I groaned and rolled over to scan the aftermath of empty bottles lying on the floor. An old red couch in the corner told me I'd passed out in the room at the top of the clubhouse. Better than the ditch I woke up in last week.

I did have a place in the compound. I just hadn't set foot in it in over eight years. This dank room and springy mattress were my home now, kind of made me miss my cozy trailer in Ashen Springs. Funny how life could change in a matter of minutes.

I lost track of how many holy men I'd heard preach about the sanctity of life. 'It's God's greatest gift,' they'd say. Fucking morons.

Anyone who looked around at this cesspool of a world would see that life wasn't a gift. It was a fucking joke. Seeking out dreams or a happy life turned into a game of *let's see how much shit we can put this guy through.'*

There were only three things people could count on:

Taxes. Uncle Sam always got his.

Shit happens. Whether you file the wrong paperwork at the DMV, lose that big promotion to Charles the suck-up, or just step on a piece of Lego, the universe will fuck with you anyway it can.

And finally, death was inevitable. Young, old, sick, and healthy, it didn't make a difference in the end.

Even in my world, these rules existed. Taxes were paid in blood. Me and my boys were the shit that happened. And death took a piece of my soul every night when I closed my eyes and saw her face.

Love, now that was the ultimate joke. Like dangling a piece of poisoned meat in front of a starving animal, we ate that shit up. Swallowed it down without so much as a second thought and then cried about our crushed soul.

My eyes landed on a half-empty whiskey bottle on the floor by the bed. May as well get an early start. Besides, I was going to need a little something to get through Church. I was not looking forward to explaining what happened at the Chinese laundry to the rest of the boys.

My only saving grace was that Tanner and Mannix were with me. Who would believe that a couple of sorority girls ran down three Reapers? I saw that shit with my own eyes and still had a hard time believing it.

It was kind of impressive, though. Hell, I was ready to give the driver props until Naomi fucking Prescott climbed out the passenger door.

I swear that bitch was put on this earth to fuck with me. I'd never wanted to hate fuck someone so bad in my life. I meant hate fuck. Pound into her hard while I watched the life fade from her eyes.

"Snide fucking bitch," I sighed and rolled out of bed.

Church stared in fifteen minutes. I better get my ass in gear.

I kicked an empty bottle and gave the room a quick scan for my pants. The glass bottle rolled across the floor and clinked off the leg of the red couch, where I spotted my jeans.

A shower could come after Church. Besides, none of the guys cared what I looked like. Hell, half of them probably smelled just as bad as I did. Then again, the scent of stale whiskey could be coming from the various bottles tossed about?

I glanced down at my dick and muttered out a string of curse words. He was full-mast and ready to go, all because I thought about that cunt.

Grumbling under my breath, I made my way across the room and snatched my jeans. One leg was in when a voice interrupted me.

"You gotta get one of the sweet butts to clean this shit up."

I stumbled forward, whacking my knee off the arm of the couch.

"Jesus fucking Christ, Beast," I growled while grimacing at the pain shooting up my thigh.

How did that big fucker move so quietly? I swear he had the grace of a goddamn cat. I sure as hell wasn't that silent, and Beast had a good sixty pounds on me.

None of which was fat, hence the road name. Arnie was his given name, which was fucking hilarious. Not as funny as Tanner's last name. Now that shit made me keel over.

Beast gave me one of his signature disgruntled huffs and crossed his arms, "Thought I better come make sure you were alive."

"You mean Jaz sent you up here," I argued.

Jaz was Beast's old lady and mother superior around here. No one and I mean no one, fucked with her. Not because they were worried about what her husband might do. She was the scary one in that relationship. Seeing as most guys were pretty attached to their nuts, they steered clear of the feisty redhead.

I liked her. She kept the sweet butts in line and wasn't afraid to go toe to toe with a drunk, angry biker. Chick had bigger balls than most of the guys around here. Even when we were kids, she wasn't afraid to kick my ass.

"I told her you were fine, but you know how she is." He stopped to roll his dark gaze around the room. "You are fine, aren't you?"

Depends on your definition of fine.

"Something wrong with a guy letting loose?"

We all liked to party. Some more than others, and me more than most. Alcohol and pussy were the only things that drowned out the voices in the back of my head.

"Uh-huh?" He grunted and kicked a bottle. "Seems like you've been doing that a lot lately."

I yanked my jeans up over my hips and turned to face him. "Your point?"

"What's your niece's name? Riley?"

"Don't fucking start."

I knew where he was going with this. Riley's mom was an alcoholic that crashed her car into a telephone pole. I may have a drink or two a night–okay, maybe more than two–but I wasn't her mother. If I was going to off myself, I'd eat the hollow point bullet I kept in my right front pocket.

Blowing my brains out the back of my skull, pretty sure that had a zero survivability rate. I even had the place picked out to do the deed, had to make things right first, though. That meant taking care of my brother and returning the Lost Souls to their rightful place.

"Look, Spider..."

"Don't call me that," I growled, "road names are earned."

I deserted my brothers and hid. I didn't deserve shit.

His brow rose. "Oh, are we playing the pity party now?"

"Shut the fuck up."

"Oh boo hoo," He whined, "little Chase lost his piece of ass..."

I was across the room, puffing my chest up against his before he could finish speaking.

"I said shut the fuck up."

"Why? You gonna hit me? Come on then." His big mitt slapped off my right cheek, taunting me to take a swing. "Do it."

"Stop it," I growled when he slapped me again.

But Beast didn't stop. He kept tapping my tapping my face until I cracked and swung my fist. Venting all the pent-up rage and anger I'd been holding back in one strike. And he took it.

Beast let my knuckles scrape across his teeth before slamming me back against the wall and pressing his forearm into my neck.

"You feel that heat burning the back of your brain?"

I did. I could feel that shit pouring through my veins like lava.

"That's anger." He leaned in, getting right in my face, "and it's the only fucking thing you should be feeling right now. Get mad, Spider, and when you've done that, get fucking pissed. Use it. Take that shit out on every motherfucker you come across until you're holding your brother's heart in your hand."

I shoved him off me and stormed across the room to grab the whiskey.

"You want to honor her memory?" He tipped his chin at the bottle in my hand, "Then stop hiding and do the job your father knew you could. Be the man she wanted you to be."

My fingers tightened around the glass neck. It was my fault she was gone. I knew she was too pure for this world, and I took her anyway.

'I made my own choices. None of this is on you.'

Yes it was. I should've stayed away. I should've...

Beast sighed. "She wouldn't want this for you."

'He's right.'

"You need to move on."

How could I move on? Without Sam, there was nothing to move on to.

'Let us go, Chase.'

"I can't," I said and lifted the bottle to my lips.

The only thing that stopped me from chugging it back was a loud bang that rang out. Both Beast and I cocked our heads at the closed bathroom door as scuffling sounds echoed through. Someone was in there.

Beast's hand was already going for his Glock. "You alone up here?"

I shook my head. Didn't think I did. then again, the last thing I remembered was getting into the whiskey.

Another crash.

"There a window in there?"

Sobriety washed over me in a hot wave of rage.

Beast pulled out his Glock while I snatched my revolver off the table and aimed at the closed door. Since I came back, Reapers had been crawling through the woodwork.

Fucking with our turf, doing drive-bys, and even breaking into the compound. Considering my brother was their Pres, a few attempts at the compound had been successful.

"Message Tanner," I said while cocking the hammer back, "tell him to go around back and cover the window."

If my brother was going to serve up one of his men on a silver fucking platter, who was I to argue?

Both Beast and I zeroed in on the doorknob as it started to turn.

"Leg shots only?" he whispered.

I nodded. "Can't question a dead man."

The door opened, and I don't know who was more shocked? Us or the topless brunette screaming?

"Shit bitch," I flinched and waved the gun at her, "can you shut your fucking yap."

Don't get me wrong, I appreciated a nice pair of bouncing tits as much as the next guy, but her shrill cries were slicing into my hungover brain.

She screamed louder, jumped back, and slammed the door. Worked for me. It at least dampened the piercing sound.

Beast shook his head and put the gun away. "Brought someone home with you last night, I take it?"

"Apparently."

No sooner had I said that then we heard Tanner's voice come from the other side.

"Well, hey there, sweetheart. I hope you're waiting for me."

Prick must've climbed in through the window.

"Fucking Playboy," Beast turned and marched out the door. "I'll tell the boys to give you a few."

I scrubbed a hand down my face. The chick was still screaming. If I didn't calm her down, Tanner wouldn't be the only fucker she had to be worried about.

Chapter 2

NAOMI

"Hey, you!" I snapped my fingers at one of the girls scrubbing my car.

Yes, I knew her name. Cammie, how much more country could you get than that? Still not as bad as my roommate. Freaking Ava. I know she roomed with the Mayberry prom queen on purpose.

Ah well, I could worry about that later. Right now, Miss Cammie was using her country muscles to wash my car. I wanted it clean, not stripped.

"Careful. That paint job is worth more than your tuition."

There was a reason I didn't let Ava drive my Mercedes. Last time, she tore the top off. I still had no idea how she did that. The top was down.

Cammie perked up and fluttered her eyes innocently. "I'm just cleaning."

Cleaning, my ass.

"I'm sure those cow wrangling muscles are useful back at the farm, but lighten up on my car."

For half a second, when the other three girls snickered, I thought she might challenge me. She had that defiant look in her eyes. Unfortunately, all she did was grumble as she hung her head.

I sighed. Sorority life wasn't supposed to be this boring. It should be more sophisticated and upper class. Not needy and naive. Never thought I'd miss Riley Adams and her smart-ass mouth.

She was just another piece of docksider trash. A nobody from a low-class neighborhood. Yet here I sat, silently hoping one of these girls would lash out at me. I may not have liked Riley, but at least she was a challenge.

Why Micha Kessler chose her, I'd never understand. That girl literally had a criminal record. Which was saying a lot considering her dad was sheriff. My dad wouldn't let me spend a minute in jail, let alone be there long enough to get a record, and she wasn't the only one.

Three of Ashen Springs' best and brightest were scooped up by lesser beings. Apparently, slumming it was the way to go back home. Though, Parker and Lana were kind of forgivable.

Seeing as she was technically a mafia princess, one might consider her in a slightly higher elevation. I could even understand Logan Hudson's choice. Shelby Grace was gorgeous. But Micha and Riley?

I glanced over at my car. Hulk version 2.0 had finally eased off. Now, I could relax. Letting out a breath, I stretched back on the lounger. Ava was always harping on me about being nicer to people.

This coming from the girl that stabbed a guy last week because he was wearing pink. While I agreed the color didn't compliment him, it was no reason to stick a knife in his gut.

On the upside, he'd probably never wear pink again. So, in reality, Ava saved us all from that fashion faux pas.

Part of me hoped I'd find more highbred girls at college. It was a sorority after all. But none of these girls were like Ava and I. They were small-time princesses, begging for guidance. More puppies to add to my collection.

I slid my sunglass over my eyes and sunk back into the warm rays. My mother got her color from the salon, whereas I preferred the natural look. Fake was her thing, not mine. Then again, I suppose that was the position for a trophy wife.

Nothing in her life was real, not even her marriage. Was any marriage? Just like these girls, Puppy was the perfect title for my mother. My flawless skin and hourglass figure were the only good things she ever did for me.

"Perfect day to soak up some sun."

Speaking of puppies...

I peeked over the rim of my sunglasses at a pair of sparkling blue eyes.

This wasn't the first time Dennis Copland stood around gawking at me. He was more my type, that much I'd give him. Well-styled blonde hair and designer labels. It was the nice guy crap that I couldn't stand.

Dennis tipped his head and gave me a smile. I couldn't help but think of someone else as I eyed the crooked curl on his lips.

Chase Mathers was an insufferable asshole, but at least the glimmer in his dark eyes was real. That didn't mean I thought he was attractive, despite what Ava said.

Just because the guy had the whole ruggedly handsome thing going on didn't mean someone like *me* would ever be interested in someone *him*. Even if he did have arms as big as my thighs.

"You going to the party this weekend?"

"No," I sighed, settled back in the lounger, and closed my eyes. "Frat parties are so last year."

High school girls got excited about drunk college guys.

"You're looking pretty good today."

Really? Was that the best he had? The way girls talked about him. I expected more. Sit down, ask me out, hell, grab my hair and kiss me. Ugh, be a man. For Christ's sake, Chase had more balls than this guy.

I could still feel his fingers around my neck, twitching with my pulse and giving me a taste of the power in those massive muscles. And they were massive.

All hard and firm bulges of might, highlighted by the ink marking his tanned skin. Pfft, whatever. He was probably all fat and flabby under that faded t-shirt.

Or he's as chiseled as a Greek god.

I grumbled under my breath and stretched my arms over my head. My mother was the one who liked to slum it.

"Is that a new suit," Dennis's annoying voice cut through my thoughts.

Ugh, is he still here.

"It looks good."

Was that supposed to be a compliment? Some line that would make me drop to my knees and beg to suck him off. Clearly, Dennis wasn't as good at this as he thought. Of course, my suit looked good. Why would I waste my time buying something that didn't.

My eyes fluttered open as I rolled my head his way. "What do you want, Dennis?"

"Well, I saw you out here," *I bet you did. Were you watching from your room with binoculars?* "and I thought you could use a refreshing drink."

Uh-huh.

I lifted my head to eye the open beer bottle in his hand. "What'd you drug it with?"

"You don't think I'd do that, do you?" His head fell back with a loud chuckle that was way too exaggerated.

"Yes."

He stood there staring at me dumbfounded for a few seconds as condensation from the bottle trickled across his fingers.

"I-I wouldn't." He stuttered out and took a long swig of the beer. "See, it's perfectly safe."

Alright, so this one wasn't drugged.

I didn't say anything, just laid my head back down. Apparently, he didn't like being ignored because the nice guy façade dropped faster than an addict ready to earn her next fix.

"I can have any girl I want. You should be honored."

Bored by his pathetic attempt at a threat, I yawned out, "Should I?"

"Careful bitch," he hissed back, "I can make or break you."

Is that what he thought?

"I'm the king around here."

I had to hold back a laugh. King around here? What kind of crap was that? Micha Kessler, Logan Hudson, and the other Knights, now those were kings. They had real power. Power I'd seen them flex numerous times.

Dennis was nothing more than a jock with a big head. I couldn't wait until he ran into Micha on campus. Now, that I wanted to be there for.

"So how about you play nice," the corner of his mouth curled, "and I'll play nice."

Dennis wanted to play? Alright. I wasn't blinded by his sparkling eyes. Nor did I give a shit if he was president of his fraternity.

I wasn't the mousy little girl in the corner he could make fold with a few words. I was a lioness, built to devour and destroy, and had no problem wiping that entitled delusion from his mind.

Because it wasn't the king who ruled.

It was fucking the queen.

"You know what," I sat up, pushed my sunglasses to the top of my head, and gave him a sweet smile, "I think we got off on the wrong foot. Why don't you come sit with me?"

Like the puppy that he was, Dennis flopped down beside me with a victorious smile. Two seconds later, his hand was running up my back.

I wanted to roll my eyes at his predictability. Instead, I slid closer and ran my hand up his thigh.

"You're right," I leaned in, bring my lips a breath away from his, "it is better when we play nice."

I held back the gag as his breath washed over my face, "I told you."

This was too easy. It was a bit disappointing. I pushed him back on the lounger and crawled over his body, straddling his thighs. Which he was all too happy to let me do. Cocky bastard even folded his hands behind his head, like he excepted me to just pop his dick in my mouth.

I went with it, taking my time to smooth my palm down his chest to the buckle of his belt.

"Is this what you want?" I purred while slipping my fingers under the waistband of his jeans.

"Yeah, Baby, this is what I want."

I reached down, wrapped my hand around the pathetic thing he called a dick and yanked. The yowl that followed made my lips curl.

"You bitch," he growled, reaching up to grab my hair.

"Uh-uh," I tsked and gave him another yank, "careful." I tipped my chin back at the girls washing my car. "My girls might come over here," I leaned in and added in a whisper, "wouldn't want them to find out how tiny your dick is."

He pulled roughly on my hair and raised his hand to slap me.

"Go ahead," I dared him. "Hit me. There's plenty of witnesses."

"Exactly," he growled back, "you're crushing my dick. No one would blame me for slapping the shit out of you."

"Am I? Or am I the girl giving you a hand job?"

Realization filled his face as he glanced around because that's exactly what it looked like. Unlike this simpleton, I knew what I was doing.

"Here's what's going to happen. You're going to leave and never talk to me or any of the other Pi Kappa girls again. Or our little rendezvous will become the hot topic on campus."

He was going to test me. I could see it in his glare. Like most of the guys I knew, Dennis didn't like backing down. Especially to a girl. Unfortunately for him, I spent years learning how to play the daddy card. I could cry on demand.

When his hold in my hair tightened, I twisted my lips and cried out, "Ouch, you're hurting me."

That worked, his hand immediately fell away as heads turned to look at us.

"You won't get away with this," he growled quietly.

Yes I would.

"Careful, I play victim real well," I pulled my hand out of his pants and leaned down to whisper in his ear, "Don't. Fuck. With. Me."

With that, I got off him and sauntered inside to wash my hand.

CHASE

The Greek letters above the door glistened in the moonlight. Standing on the porch of a frat house in the middle of the night was not a place I expected to be. Can't say I was too surprised either.

Most of the campuses were Reaper territory. Though, we'd been slowly reclaiming them, we had just as many dealers in this one as they did. Most of ours we turned from their side.

Jax's supplier wasn't too happy to find out what went down. The Reapers had more men than us, but the Lost Souls' connections ran deep. Not to mention, loyalty was important in our world. How much could you trust a man that turned on his own brother?

Now, we had the superior product, and more than half of his former customers. Problems came with this part of the business. Drugs attracted the wrong kind of people.

Like the sketchy fuck inside that thought he could get away

without paying. Tanner and Mannix were inside having a *'chat'* with him.

The door vibrated as a loud crash rolled through the other side. Beast, who was by the front steps leading up to the porch, didn't so much as twitch. He just stood there with his arms crossed and a grumpy fucking look on his face.

"Where you going, Chet?" I heard Mannix say from the other side of the door, followed by Tanner's snicker. "We were just starting to have fun."

I snorted and shook my head. Fucking Chet. Who named their kid that?

Everything went quiet after a couple sounds that I was pretty sure were slaps. An open palm hit had a distinctive clack that a fist didn't. I doubted that was why shit calmed down in the house.

If anything, shit was getting worse. Tanner and Mannix got off on fucking with people. My guess was, they dragged Chet off to have some *'fun,'* as Tanner put it.

Sam knew what I did. I never hid that part of my life from her. That didn't mean she agreed with it. She never asked me to quit. I don't think that thought even traveled through her mind once. She simply accepted me for who I was.

The only thing she did request was that I took it easy on dumb fucks like Chet, said that I should give them the chance to see the error of their ways without so many broken bones and bruises.

Problem was, broken bones and bruises was the only language I spoke.

'You have a soft side, Chase. I've seen it.'

Ignoring the voice, I leaned back against the stone wall and plucked out the cigarette I had resting behind my ear.

'Think about Riley.'

My brows furrowed as I tried to concentrate on the smoke I was twirling between my fingers.

'What would she say if she knew what you were letting them do in there?'

Riley wouldn't say anything. She'd kick my ass, and then probably Tanners. My niece was a tiny little thing, but I taught her well. She didn't take shit, even from me. She took shit from Micha Kessler, though. That prick was involved with darker shit than I was.

I couldn't help but wonder if it was my fault she fell in love with him? Did my broken soul taint hers?

'Riley loves you.'

"That's the problem."

"What?" Beast asked, arching his brow over his shoulder.

"Nothing."

This was the third time Beast caught me talking to myself. Which I was doing because Sam wasn't here giving me advice to steer me on the right path. She was fucking dead. Cold and buried in a box in the ground next to our son.

Beast tipped his head. "Do I need to be worried about you?"

Probably.

Luckily, I didn't have to explain anything because the perfect distraction came stumbling up the walk.

"I think you should be more worried about him." I arched my brow at the lace thong the drunk idiot was wearing as a hat. Guess he got lucky.

That or he just got back from a panty raid. I think they still did that shit in college? Mind you, the only experience I had to go off of was from movies.

Beast muttered a "What the fuck?" while scrubbing a hand down his face.

Sure the kid looked like a fool, but I'd seen worse. Tanner wore a bright pink tutu to Riley's school just to make the crotchety receptionist smile. She didn't. I don't think that old bitch was capable of it.

Most people were surprised to find out the Dupire twins were related to her. Other than Marnie being quiet, neither one of her granddaughters had a thing in common with her.

I wonder if Riley knew?

"Did I miss a costume party?" The drunk idiot laughed and tripped up the steps while waving his finger at Beast's cut. "That's some good shit. It looks real."

Neither Beast nor I said a thing. We just cocked a brow.

"Okay?" He muttered while swinging his gaze from one to the other. "Not big talkers, I guess."

Again we said nothing.

"Right. Well, if you don't mind." He motioned past Beast's huge body to the door behind him.

"Fuck off," was Beast's response. "Frat's closed."

Beast was a grumpy motherfucker. It didn't take much to agitate him. When the kid lifted his finger and jabbed it into his chest, I knew his night was done.

"Hey man, you can't…"

That's all the dimwit got out before a giant fist swung through the air, clacking off his jaw. He flew back, landing on the grass unconscious.

I glanced over at the two others bodies crumpled up in the corner of the deck. They were knocked out earlier. To be fair, one decided to be a smart ass and throw a tantrum by kicking our bikes. Fucker was lucky he wasn't dead.

As Beast lifted the kid's limp body, I lifted the cigarette to my nose and took a deep inhale, sucking back the rich scent. Fuck, that smelled good. It'd been eight years since I had a smoke.

That was one bad habit I'd so far managed to avoid falling back into. Not sure why I carried one around? I felt better knowing it was there, I guess, kind of like a security blanket.

A chick's voice carried through the breeze so loud I expected to see her standing right in front of me.

"Get your asses moving girls."

When I looked up, I saw a tiny blonde across the street with a megaphone held to her mouth. A sense of familiarity washed over me as I eyed her pink Care Bear pajamas.

It was possible I knew her. I spent most nights drunk and buried in pussy I'd forget the next day. It dawned on me when a row of girls came shuffling out the door.

No fucking way.

I pushed off the wall and sauntered over to stand next to Beast, who was also staring at what I assumed was a sorority house.

"That's the crazy bitch that ran down the Reapers."

"Really?" His eyes shifted my way. "Which one?"

I tipped my chin at the blonde directing the other girls. "The little one."

I assumed this was some hazing thing based on their yawning faces and sleepwear.

"Fuck off," Beast waved his hand, "that chick can't weigh more than ninety pounds."

"Weight doesn't matter much when the car is the weapon."

He huffed out a grunt, and we sat back to watch things play out.

Personally, I didn't trust the chick. I could've let it go if she had just ran down one and kept going. We were in the middle of a gunfight. That sort of thing should be terrifying to civilians, but this bitch came back, and not for one, but all three.

Even drove into the Chinese laundry to get the last one. That kind of crazy shouldn't be walking the streets.

"Fuck me," I muttered when the last girl came strutting out of the house in a forest green silk top and matching shorts.

Naomi, I should've fucking known.

Seeing her prance outside with her head held high caused my jaw to clench. There was no way she just rolled out of bed. The other girls had droopy eyes and messy hair, while Naomi's golden hair flowed in perfect waves down her back.

My eyes narrowed on her long thick lashes, fluttering as she rolled her eyes. Was she wearing make-up? What did she do? Make everyone wait while she dolled herself up.

"Selfish cunt," I grumbled as she climbed up on one of the milk crates.

"Who?"

I ignored Beast and kept my eyes on Naomi. It was annoying how graceful she was. One fluid bend of her long leg, and she was up with the rest of them. The girl moved like a fucking panther. Everything about her was smooth, calm, and poised. Except her face, which was currently wound tightly in her ever-present bitch scowl.

Fuck, I hated her. My dick, however, did not. She'd been out here one minute, and I was already getting hard.

I glanced down at the unlit cigarette in my hand and said, "fuck it," before placing it between my lips.

The lighter was barely out of my pocket when Beast reached over and snatched it out of my mouth.

"What the fuck?"

"I'm not letting you start this shit again?" His giant mitt fisted around the smoke, crushing it. "Your drinking is bad enough."

"Who are you." I growled back at him, "my fucking father?"

"How's this for some fatherly advice?" his hand lifted, smacking me on the back of the head. "Pull your head out of your ass."

I glared at him while rubbing my head. Fucker.

"Don't go doing stupid shit like smoking because you have a hard-on for some chick."

"I do not have a hard-on for that bitch," I argued as I rolled my eyes up Naomi's long shapely legs.

Beast snorted in disagreement. Whatever. I suppose to the average guy, Naomi was bangable. Provided she didn't open her mouth. I tipped my head at the row of girls. This might be a blessing in disguise.

The entire purpose of hazing was to humiliate the new recruits. Every group, club, and society did it in some form, including mine. Maybe I'd finally get to see queen bitch knocked off her high horse? Now that sounded like fun.

I cocked my hip against the railing and crossed my arms as the crazy one spouted out questions. For a tiny thing, she was demanding. I was a bit surprised no one stood up to her.

Then again, she did give three Reapers a fatal case of road rash. God fucking knew what she did to those girls.

The game, which appeared to be a question and answer one, carried on. If the girls on the crates got an answer wrong or didn't say anything, they had to down a shot.

"This is what passes for hazing these days?" Beast shook his head.

I grunted in agreement, didn't seem very difficult to me. Worst case scenario, they got drunk. Big deal, I did that shit every night.

By the tenth round, half the girls were falling down. Much to my dismay, Naomi wasn't one of them. In fact, she hadn't gotten a single question wrong, and there were some hard ones. Like what was the airspeed velocity of an unladen swallow?

What the fuck was that? She had to be cheating. I glared at Naomi, standing there staring at her nails as if she was bored. Now, that shit I could put a stop to.

With a smirk on my face, I skipped down the steps. Let's see how bored the princess is when I make things more difficult for her.

Tanner and Mannix must've come out just as I started walking away because I heard Mannix's growly tone rumbled behind me.

"Where the fuck is he going?"

"Who cares. You see that shit," Tanner sang, "it's like an outdoor slumber party, and I am so down for a pillow fight."

Did I care if Tanner followed me? Not one bit. I was willing to bet it wasn't just him following me either. Especially when the girls' eyes widened. They all looked shocked and terrified, except Naomi, who rolled her eyes, and the little crazy one.

"Hey, I remember you guys," crazy chick sang, "did you bring me spring rolls?"

Tanner of course, jumped all over that shit. "I'll bring you all the spring rolls you want, Baby."

"Not you. I don't like you."

I held back a chuckle as Tanner sucked in a gasp.

"What did I do?"

She stood back and eyed him for a second. "Your hair's too long."

Beast and Mannix burst out laughing, and I swear I could hear Tanner's jaw drop. I didn't care what they were doing. There was one sole purpose I had for coming over here, and that purpose was glaring at me so intensely, I could feel the hatred rolling off her.

"Hey, Princess," I rolled my eyes down the length of her. She did look good standing up there, that much I'd give her. Tipping my chin at her nipples hard against the thin silk fabric, I added, "happy to see me?"

Without a word, Naomi stepped down off her pedestal and stalked over. I thought for sure she was going to say something snarky or get in my face. I was completely unprepared for what she did next.

Naomi reached out, palmed my dick through my jeans, and leaned in to whisper, "Seems like you're the happy one here."

I was so consumed by the warmth of her hand on my cock, that I almost didn't hear the low rumble in the distance. Over Naomi's shoulder, I could see the shadows of four bikes coming down the street, and they weren't mine.

Mannix was the first of the others to notice. His 9mm was in his hand before I pushed Naomi out of the way and yelled at Beast, "Get them inside."

Beast sprang to action, barking loudly at the girls, who hustled to run through the door. But there wasn't time for all of them to get inside before shots rang out.

Bullets whizzed through the air, slicing in the ground and cutting through the house as Mannix joined Beast, pushing girls behind anything they could use for cover.

Tanner and I marched forward, popping off shots as the bikes whizzed by. We might've gotten one or two if that crazy little chick hadn't run up and chucked her shoe. Though she did nail a Reaper in the head, causing him to skid slightly, Tanner had to grab her and shield her from the incoming gunfire.

It was hard enough to concentrate with all these chicks screaming. Unlike us, whose first priority was to make sure the girls were okay, the Reapers would shoot every one of them to get at me. Which was exactly why I couldn't concentrate and get a good shot off before they were fading into the darkness.

All I could picture was Riley staring at me accusingly as she was riddled with bullets. Still, I stepped out onto the street and popped off a few more shots at the shadows in the distance.

That's when a red BMW pulled up.

My first instinct was to aim at the driver, which I did for half a second. Adrenaline pumped through my heart at a wild pace as my finger readied on the trigger. I calmed down when he stepped out.

The only guy I knew that wore a jean jacket like that was Preston Whitley.

The prick was lucky I recognized him, otherwise, he would've been welcomed by a hail of bullets. Mannix and Beast also had their guns aimed this way. Tanner was too busy struggling with crazy to worry about anything else.

I held up a hand, telling the others to back down as Preston nodded at me and sauntered around the trunk of his car. My brows furrowed at his calm acceptance of the situation, and then arched when he slammed the trunk shut and snapped an M-40 together.

Who the fuck carries a sniper rifle in their car?

Preston propped the gun on the hood, aimed it down the street, and looked through the scope. "You want him alive?"

"Uh, yeah?" I said, not really sure what else to say.

One shot. That's all it took for that motherfucker to take out a bike. The back tire spun out, flipping the bike and driver back on the road behind him. One of the Reapers stopped, probably to help his fallen compadre.

A second later, a bullet cut through his helmet, exploding the back of his skull on the ground. Any thought the other two had of coming back vanished after that. They kicked their bikes into gear and rolled down the street.

Mannix swung his gun through the air. "Who the fuck is this guy."

"Preston!" Crazy chick rushed over and threw her arms around Preston.

He rolled his eyes and half-heartedly hugged her back.

"Did daddy send you?"

Huh, so she was his sister. Made sense, I guess. I didn't know the kid that well, but anyone who looked at him could tell there wasn't much of a soul in that body.

"Cops will be here soon." Preston's cold grey eyes locked on mine. "You should go."

I couldn't agree more. Nodding at my boys, I turned and headed for my bike.

"Seriously," Mannix said, following. "Who the fuck is that guy?"

Chapter 4

NAOMI

I had to hand it to Preston. By the time the cops showed, there was absolutely no sign of Chase or his lackeys. He walked over to the dead body, took his gun, and shot up his car.

After which, he lit the bikes on fire and drug his leg on the ground so he'd have injuries to match his story about diving behind his car.

He even threatened the girls to keep their mouths shut, though I doubted any of them would say shit. Especially after he kicked the door in to the frat house across the street and came out with a rolled-up rug, which he stashed in Ava's smashed-up car around back.

It was unnerving to see him in action, and I grew up with the guy. Thankfully the cops bought his story about those guys just opening fire. He didn't seem very impressed when they took his rifle, though I suspected he'd have it back by the end of the day.

"Do you think they'll come back?" Bailey asked.

I shrugged and sighed at my mayberry roommate. Bailey had her brown hair in pigtails today. Freaking pigtails. At least it matched the plaid shirt she was wearing.

She clutched the end of her shirt and swung her light eyes my way. "What do we do if they do?"

"Don't worry, Ava has a closet full of shoes," I glared over my magazine at Ava, who was sitting in the big pink chair across the room, twirling her hair. "I'm sure she'll run them off."

Her big grey eyes swung my way. "What?"

"Did you get your shoe back?"

"Oh yeah," She nodded, "Pressy brought it back for me."

Preston, who happened to be walking by, paused long enough to shift his gaze Ava's way and shook his head.

Cammie leaned over and whispered, "Is there something wrong with him?"

"You have no idea," I snorted.

"I think he's cute." Macy, one of the senior girls, sighed dreamily. "I wonder if he has a girlfriend?"

Have fun with that, Macy.

A lot of the guys I grew up with were manwhores. I assumed Preston was as well, though I'd only known a few girls he'd been with, and they were never the same after. Silas and Micha were the only exceptions to this. Silas's massive cock detoured a lot of girls. And I meant Massive.

I saw it once. Something as thick as a soda can should not go in someone's body. There wasn't enough money in the world to make me go near that thing.

Unlike the rest, Micha chose not to sleep around. There were three or four girls he stuck to for the most part. I used to be one of them. Not because I particularly enjoyed fucking him, it was a status thing.

There was a certain order to things. Outcasts stuck together, beautiful people belonged with beautiful people, and the head cheerleader dated the quarterback, who was typically king of the school. That wasn't the case in Ashworth. Sean Callaghan was quarterback, but Micha was king.

"Seriously!" Bailey clutched onto Cammie's arm. "What if they come back?"

Ugh.

Tired of all their overreactions, I got up and stormed out. A couple of thugs pulled a drive-by. So what if someone got shot – which no one did. If they couldn't handle this, the real world was going to eat them alive.

This was nothing. I stared in the face of true evil when I was four years old, and it was nothing like what people thought. The monster of the story was sometimes more beautiful than the hero. My monster had stunning green eyes...

"Hi there."

I smacked some more sand in my bucket and looked up at a pair of bright green eyes. I liked them. They twinkled like gems on Mommy's jewelry. Sometimes she'd let me play with her necklaces, but only if she was there and I was very careful. They were 'spensive she said. I'm not sure what she meant, but she said the same thing about the vase I broke. I got in a lot of trouble for that.

"You're Naomi, right?"

My nose scrunched up at him. "I'm aposed to talk to strangers."

Mommy and Daddy told me never to go anywhere or talk to anybody they didn't know cause strangers were sometimes bad.

"You're Ava's friend, aren't you?" I nodded as he sat down on the edge of the sandbox. "Ava's my friend too, which means I'm not a stranger."

That made sense, I guess. Ava was my best friend, and she wasn't a bad person. I looked up at the man's golden hair shinning in the sunlight. The monsters in my stories were yucky and gross. This man didn't seem scary.

I carefully tipped my bucket over and tapped the bottom before slowly lifting it up. Everything stayed how I wanted it, except the top, which crumpled apart.

"Stupid castle," I grumbled and smacked the rest of the pile.

The man picked up one of my shovels and tipped his head. "Want some help?"

"I don't know." I stopped to eye him. "How come you're at the park."

I heard mommy talking to daddy once about someone who was here without a kid. She called him creepy, and I didn't like creepy things.

"My son's over there." He nodded at a little boy chasing girls around the swings with a stick.

"Logan!" I squealed. "I know Logan. He pulls my hair."

The man chuckled, "That's boys for you."

"I don't like boys."

"Wanna know a secret," he leaned in and whispered, "I don't like boys either."

I giggled. He was funny, and since he was Logan's dad, mommy must know him. So it would be okay to let him play with me.

"Okay, Mr. Logan's Dad, you can help me."

He smiled and said, "Call me Ryker..."

I ROUNDED the corner to the kitchen. The marble counters weren't as nice as the ones in my house. About what I expected. Higher than middle class, but not quite top of the line. Much like the rest of the house.

The furniture was last year's line, the wallpaper was outdated, and the floors scuffed from lack of waxing. They really needed to hire better cleaning staff, if they had any at all.

Sauntering over to the fridge, I grabbed a bottle of water and cracked it open. The hot Miami sun pouring in through the windows made me briefly consider going for a tan.

The bullet-riddled front yard wasn't exactly appealing, though. That wouldn't be fixed until next week. Yet another reason to hate Chase Mathers.

No one was around. I could sneak out back for a smoke. I didn't do it often and certainly not where anyone could see–ladies didn't smoke, but right now, I could really use one.

The idea died when Preston stepped through the back door at the same time two girls joined me in the kitchen. The girls huddled up in the corner while Preston stuck his head in the fridge.

"You got any beer in this place?"

"We're not supposed to have alcohol in the house."

Preston closed the fridge door and leaned against it. "I didn't ask what you're supposed to do."

"I think there's a bottle of wine over there." I tipped my chin at the top cupboard next to where the girls were huddled.

I rolled my eyes at their giggles and hushed whispers when Preston headed for the cupboard. Their obvious attraction was so obvious it was pathetic. What really got my attention was Preston's reaction. He didn't even look at them.

Come to think of it, I hadn't seen him look twice at any of the girls here, and a few of them I'd fuck. Don't get me wrong, on a good day, Preston was cold, but even he had urges. I wondered if this had anything to do with that frumpy girl I saw him watching downtown?

Apparently, one of the girls decided to make a move because she slowly tiptoed closer to Preston as he opened the wine and took a swig. I think this one's name was Iris. Hadn't really talked to either of them, nor did I care to.

They arrived two days ago and stuck pretty much to themselves.

"I have some vodka in my room." She dipped her eyelashes, giving him a demure take-me look. "It's not beer, but it's better than wine."

When Preston didn't respond, she lifted her hand and danced her fingers up his arm. He paused, holding the mouth of the bottle against his lips as his eyes shifted to her hand.

Iris took his look as an opening. A smile spread across her face, and I internally shook my head.

"I could share it with you."

"The next time you touch me," he swallowed back a mouthful of wine, "I'll cut your fucking hand off."

A triad of emotions flashed across Iris's face. Confusion, disbelief, and uncertain humor. When horror sparked in her eyes, draining her complexion of color, I knew she got it.

Preston wasn't joking or threatening her. He meant every word he said. I didn't just know this, I'd witnessed it a couple of times. Preston and Ava were twins, but Preston was born fucked up. Ava was destroyed.

"Let's go." Iris's friend grabbed her arm and pulled her out of the room, leaving me alone with Preston.

A scary position to some, none of whom grew up watching Ava's mind deteriorate.

Sometimes, I thought my friendship with her was the only thing that saved me from her brother. We'd butted heads on more than one occasion. And no, that wasn't why I was friends with her.

We had a special kind of bond, one forged in misery and blood. Not unlike prisoners of war. Ava was my best friend because she was the only person in this world who truly understood me. Not even my own parents knew what we went through.

I looked over at Preston as he polished off the bottle. "Feel better?"

He didn't say anything, just tossed the bottle in the sink and crossed his arms. This was why we didn't get along. Preston wasn't the kind of person I'd have deep conversations with, but him ignoring me was just plain rude.

"Why are you even here?"

His grey eyes rolled up to meet mine. "Because someone decided to let my sister mow down a bunch of people."

"Yeah, right," I snickered, "like anyone lets Ava do anything."

"If anyone had a chance at stopping her, it would be you." He pushed off the counter and stalked my way. "Did you even try?"

"No, Preston, I begged your sister to drive into a gunfight because I had nothing better to do," I marched forward to meet him, "like, I don't know, live perhaps."

"Don't get smart with me, Naomi," Preston puffed his chest up and stepped into my space. "Unlike my sister, I don't give a shit if you're around."

Now that was an empty threat. As much as Preston hated me, he also cared about his sister. I don't know if I'd call it love. I wasn't entirely sure if he was capable of that emotion. But it was as close as a guy like him could get.

"Go home, Preston," I sighed and spun for the door. "I'm sure your church girl misses you."

That's when everything took a turn. Preston's fingers dug into my arm as he slammed me back so hard the knobs of the stove dug into my tailbone.

"What the fuck did you just say to me?"

I didn't know what to say. The look in his eyes had me stunned. They weren't the vacant grey orbs of nothingness I was used to, the blue fleck hidden in the pale color danced with emotion, and not a good one. For the first time in my life, I was scared of Preston Whitley.

"Let's get one thing straight," he leaned in, getting his face right in mine, "I don't give a fuck what you think you're the queen of or who your daddy is. If you go anywhere near Marnie Dupire, I will gut you and leave your body on daddy's front doorstep. Do you understand?"

His eyes narrowed in warning, which was when I shoved him back.

"Fuck off, Preston. I don't give a shit about your church mouse," I snarled and pranced out. "Go back home and skin her alive for all I care."

No one pushed me around. Not even Preston Whitley. I wasn't anyone's victim. That vulnerable little girl died a long time ago.

'I want my mommy.'

Ava wrapped her arms around me. 'It's okay, Naomi, I'll protect you.'

'Aww, sweet little Ava, just like her daddy," the green-eyed monster laughed. "Self-sacrifice didn't win him any prizes, little girl.'

I shook away the memory and walked down the hall to where I could hear the other girls. Excited voices and giggles filled the air, making me let out a breath.

It seemed the gloom and doom in the atmosphere had finally left. Good, I could use a pick me up.

A pick me up was not what I got. In the middle of the room, on the oak coffee table, was a large vase of lilies and daisies.

The flowers themselves were beautiful and lightened up the room. It was what Cammie said that caused my brow to arch.

"I can't believe he sent us flowers, and the note is so sweet."

"They did kind of put our lives in danger," Bailey bent over and took a deep inhale of the flowers before smiling back at Cammie, "but they did save us too."

My face dropped. You've got to be kidding me.

"Give me that." I snarled, snatching the note out of Cammie's hand.

Dear girls,

We're so sorry for the trouble we caused and are glad no one was hurt. Please know it was never our intention to put you in danger. Anyone of my boys would happily take a bullet to keep you safe. Please let me know if there is anything we can do for you. You can find me at the clubhouse in the marshes by the old amusement park.

Sincerely,
Chase Mathers

Bailey's bright eyes sparkled at me. "Isn't that sweet?"

"No, it's not sweet! This asshole brought his shit to our front door, and you think a few flowers are going to make it alright? What the hell is wrong with you?"

They all stood there staring at me with wide eyes. Bailey's mouth moved with lost words while Cammie stammered out, "Well... I mean... they weren't the ones shooting..."

"No," my finger flew up, cutting her off in a firm point, "don't excuse them. Actually, you know what," I stormed over, snatched the vase of flowers off the table, and stormed out the door.

"Where are you going?" Cammie called after me.

"To deliver them back to their owner."

Right in his fucking face.

Chapter 5

CHASE

"Stop pulling my daughter into your crap!"

"Shut the fuck up, Derek," I snarled into my phone, "I'm not pulling Riley in shit."

"What do you think she's going to do when she hears about this?"

"And how's she going to hear about it?" He was lucky he wasn't here, or I'd beat the attitude out of him. "The cops have no clue we were even there."

Something I would've thanked Preston for if I didn't want to knock his teeth in. The only reason I was having this conversation was because Dean Whitley chewed out Derek for his daughter getting shot at, which I assumed Preston told him about.

The fucking Order of Ravens and Wolves. Pompous fucks with their noses stuck in the air. I'd take my club over that bullshit any day.

"Micha goes to that school," Derek shot back at me.

Speaking of pompous fucks…

Micha Kessler was next in line to lead the Order. Yeah, I kept my eye on them, just like I would any crooked bastard. Probably knew more about them than Riley's friend Marnie, and she'd dug up some pretty good dirt.

The difference between her investigation and mine was I knew how criminals thought.

I just about hung up on my niece's stepbrother when he told me my bloodline was part of their society. Why the fuck would I care? Then he informed me that I had a right to vote.

So, Tanner and I rolled back into town. Not to make sure things went the way Riley wanted, but to fuck up their perfect, pristine order. Of course, things didn't go as planned. I got… distracted…

TANNER and I cocked a brow at the fountain to our left and then the house on the right. Derek's wife's house. I wouldn't call it his house because he didn't come from shit, and someone who owned a place this big, came from breeding stock better than his low rent ass.

Or they earned it in some unscrupulous manner. In my experience, people who had money didn't get it selling kittens on a street corner.

While Paisley was the kind of woman who'd rescue stray animals, her first husband was the kind of prick that would watch them burn. Ryker Hudson would've poured the gasoline and tossed the match himself, all while making his wife witness her furry friends suffer.

That guy gave new meaning to the term sick fuck.

"Cheer up," Tanner slapped his hand on my back, "we get to see our girl."

That was true. I missed my niece, talked to Riley almost every day.

"Should we knock?"

I answered him by throwing the door open. We didn't need to fucking knock. This was Riley's house. Besides, seeing me saunter in like I owned the place would piss Derek off, and I was all about that shit.

Tanner's gaze shifted around as he whistled, "Nice digs."

"If you say so," I snorted.

None of this fancy shit impressed me. Hardwood floors were still floors, and marble countertops were nothing more than polished up slabs of stone. Why waste the money when there were rocks outside and trees in the back?

"How many rooms you think they got in this place?"

I headed for the kitchen, where I could hear voices, "Too many."

One good thing about Derek's upgrade in social standing was that Riley could now get the education she deserved. I told her to take advantage of that. She whined and complained, but uptight schools like Ashworth had their advantages.

She'd get options other people didn't simply because she graduated from there. Provided her boyfriend didn't get in the way. Micha Kessler. I'd like to shove that boy's nuts down his throat.

The Kesslers were a powerful family and the head of the Order of Ravens and Wolves. I was apparently the last of the wolves side. Whatever the fuck that meant?

That's why I was here, to cast my vote for some crap initiation bullshit. Not because I gave a fuck about the Order, but because by claiming my right to vote, I'd put a chink in their perfect, pristine chain.

"You have to get her something nice."

That high-pitched tone caused me to grumble under my breath. Of course, Naomi Prescott was here. How else was fate going to fuck with me?

I couldn't get that snide little sneer out of my head. Let's not even get started on how many times I jerked it to the image of her bent over my counter.

A pair of sparkling green eyes met mine as we entered the kitchen.

Speaking of shoving someone's balls down their throat.

"Nice," Logan Hudson's lips curled, "got it."

His smile spread as the two blondes bitching at him turned and looked at us.

My gaze narrowed on Logan and then Naomi. He was the one that called me here. If this fucker planned this shit, I wasn't just going to feed him his nuts. I was gonna make him swallow the whole damn package.

"Damn," Tanner was more focused on the smaller one wearing some fancy jeans and heels. "I'm definitely a fan of the kitchen."

Her brow rose. "Is that your attempt at flirting?"

"Depends, is it working?"

The blonde sauntered forward, exaggerating the sway in her hips. Tanner was too blinded to notice that the bitch was up to no good. I could've knocked some sense into him, but why?

Cocky prick deserved whatever was coming. Fuck, most times, all he had to do was smile, and they were begging at his feet. It'd be nice to see him get shot down.

"Are you gonna give it to me, good, big boy?" she purred while dragging her finger down his chest.

Stupid fuck stepped in closer to her. "Oh yeah, baby, I'll give it to you good."

The only warning he got before her fist landed in his gut, was a tiny smirk.

"I'm going to find Logan a suit," she sang and flipped her hair over her shoulder before strutting out of the room, leaving Tanner behind in a hunched-over heap.

"Fuck," he coughed. "I think I'm in love."

"You might want to stay away from that one," Logan warned, "She's psycho."

Tanner beamed back at him. "I like psycho."

Idiot.

I crossed my arms and glared back at Naomi. She could emphasize the curl in her lip all she wanted, but I saw her checking me out, staring hard at the ridges underneath my t-shirt. When I flexed my pecks just a little, her gaze snapped back up to mine.

"Can I help you?" she snarled.

"Still mouthy, I see." I took a second to enjoy the red fabric wrapped around her curves. She'd look real good bouncing on my cock. Too bad she was an utter cunt. "Does Daddy know you're out this late?"

Her only response was to lift her chin and strut out of the room. "I should go help, Ava."

"You do that," I growled over my shoulder.

Did she think ignoring me would piss me off? That I'd chase her down? This wasn't fucking high school.

Logan hunched over, laughing. "That shit was fucking great."

I couldn't help but shake my head. Here I was in Derek Adams's house with two idiots. One bent over in amusement, and the other groaning because a little girl hit him. All this so I could cast my vote for some stupid shit I didn't give a fuck about.

How did my life turn out this way? I actually kind of missed that prissy bitch Naomi. At least with her, I could appreciate the view.

A thought I'd come to regret later when I got conned into a double date, and I kissed her. I just wanted to shut her the fuck up. Instead, I couldn't get the way she tasted out of my mind.

Fucking peaches shouldn't be so erotic.

"You remember Micha? Riley's boyfriend." Derek sang, pulling me back from the memory. "Do you know who he is?"

How could I forget? That prick was the whole reason I came back to the club. My niece was kidnapped because some sick fuck wanted to torment Micha and his crew of assholes.

"Yeah, I know who he fucking is. Did you forget who I am?" My criminal enterprise was the whole reason he disowned his sister.

"I know who you were. But you're not that guy anymore, are you? What does your club have now, fifteen maybe twenty full-fledged members?"

I sighed because he was right.

Once upon a time, the Lost Souls meant something. We ruled this city and these streets. No one, and I mean no one, did anything in Miami without us knowing. On any given night, there'd be fifty to a hundred men in the clubhouse.

Now we were lucky to pull in twenty. The rockers on the back of these cuts should be worn with age, not clean and new, which most were. I could count the number of diamond one percent patches on one hand. It was a sad time for the Lost Souls, and one that was completely my fault.

"Micha's not going to say anything."

"You don't know that," Derek growled. "He tells her all kinds of shit…"

"Yeah, did he tell her what happened to her mother?"

That shut him up. As it should. Micha had his sights set on my niece at a young age. According to their society laws, he needed a contract signed by Derek to officially claim her, which Derek's first wife was tortured to get. I may not be a good man.

Fuck, I probably had more blood on hands than Preston did–and that kid should be dripping blood–but if some prick did that shit to my wife, he wouldn't be around to breathe another day.

'You talk a big game son,' my old man chuckled in the back of my head, 'but your brother is still out there, breathing the same air.'

Rage fisted my hand on the table. *His time will come.*

'When? After you've completely destroyed my club?'

Jax did that.

'No, Chase, you did. You abandoned them when they needed you most.'

I swallowed back the guilt welling up in my chest and looked over at Tanner, who was flirting with a couple of sweet butts. In eight years, that kid never left my side. I used to tell him to fuck off and go home. Know what he said? Home was wherever I was.

My gaze swung over to Beast and his old lady playing a game of darts, then to Mannix who was perched across the room watching everyone. The three of them never lost faith in me.

I was dead to two and hiding with another, and what did they do when I called them in for backup? They got on their bikes and rolled into Ashen Springs. No questions or blame, just the bond of brother-hood. They deserved a better leader than me.

"Are you listening to me?" Derek yelled in my ear.

I was so done with this bullshit. The only reason I answered the phone was because I thought something might've happened to Riley.

"Don't you have another kid, now?" I hissed. "Maybe you should go worry about her before she winds up worse than the first daughter you neglected."

I could feel his hatred pouring in from the other end. "You don't get to lecture me about parenting. My kid's still alive."

Ice poured through my veins as my entire body went completely ridgid.

"I'm going to do you a favor, Derek, and forget you said that. Now,

I suggest you hang up before you open your yap and say something I can't forget."

"My sister…"

"I mean it, Derek," I growled. "Don't go there. You're the one that gave up on her, not me."

There were a lot of things I'd do for my niece, but if he kept pushing me, I'd make her an orphan.

"Fine," he snarled like the little bitch he was, "but for the record, I never gave up on her. I just knew you'd get her killed."

With that, he hung up.

I sat there for a second, letting the rage burn through me until I couldn't take it anymore. With a loud roar, I shot out of my chair and flipped the table over.

The fun around me came to a grinding halt as wide eyes turned my way. I could feel them judging me, heard their thoughts drifting through the air. Has he finally lost it? Maybe this time, he'd actually pull the trigger.

Traitor.

Coward.

Widower.

"Fucking Jax!" I yelled and kicked over another table.

Everybody was staring at me, and it was so quiet I could hear the clink of dishes being washed in the back. That did nothing to calm my mood.

"What the fuck are you all doing, get out there!"

Within seconds they were all bustling to get out the door. All but three. Beast, Mannix, and Tanner.

"I want three Reaper's heads on my table by midnight," I called out after them.

Beast crossed his arms. "What are you doing?"

"What you wanted me to do," I said, looking him right in the eyes. "I'm taking charge."

If my brother wanted a war, I'd give him a fucking war. Tonight the streets would rain with Reaper blood.

Chapter 5

NAOMI

The air was filled with a grinding growl as a pack of bikes swerved around my car. At least twenty men in leather roared down the street, slicing around me like water through rocky edges at the bottom of the bluffs back home.

My eyes narrowed on the last few as they passed by. More specifically, the scythe and crossbones patch stitched into the back of their vest. Lost Souls on the top with Miami Chapter 11 on the bottom. Of course, they were Chase's boys.

"Hey," I rolled down my window, stuck my head out, and yelled back at them, "watch where you're going."

One of the riders in the back glanced over his shoulder and flipped me off.

"You're lucky I have something to do, but I'm writing down your license plate number."

The smug bastard not only laughed as if my threat meant nothing, but he swept his hand over the back of his bike, where the plate was attached. To which I took a note of in my phone.

My virtual assistant was great for stuff like that. Don't know what I was going to do with his plate number, but you can bet your ass I was gonna do something.

Damned bikers thought they owned the street.

Oh, but I'm sure if one of these assholes hit my car, I'd get a nice bouquet of flowers the next day. They weren't even good ones. Lilies and daisies. Could you get more mediocre than that?

The lilies I could live with, they were kind of pretty, but moms and little sisters got daisies. Chase probably didn't even pick them out. He probably sent one of his lackeys, like the idiot that flipped me off.

"Flip me off," I muttered and settled back into my leather seat to crank up the radio. "I'll show him."

I concentrated on the road and put the incident out of my mind. The music helped a little. Normally it'd be *Taylor Swift*, or *Dua Lipa*, blaring through my speakers, something that was on-trend. I did have a reputation to keep, after all.

When I was alone, I could listen to the stuff I really liked, Classic rock. When I was little, I used to dance and sing along with gardeners while they worked, until daddy reminded me that girls didn't listen to rock.

If he knew about my secret collection, I'd have never heard the end of it. *'Proper girls don't give people a reason to judge them.'*

So, I hid my records, tapes, and digital music files. Bands from the seventies, eighties, and nineties. They were my dirty little secret. *ACDC*, a little *Metallica*. Right now, it was *Credence Clearwater Revival*, because as far as Chase Mathers was concerned, there was a 'Bad Moon Rising.'

What kind of person chose to live out here? I passed two swamps in this old rundown part of the city, and I'm pretty sure there was a serial killer living in that decrepit amusement park.

There was a car graveyard in the back and some discarded shoes on the ground. How did I know this? Because I took a wrong turn and spent twenty minutes trying to find my way out of the rusty junkyard. Even GPS avoided this part of Miami.

At least I knew I was going the right way now if the sea of leather that just drove past me didn't tell me that, then the row of bikes on the other side of a chain-link fence sure as hell did.

I steered my Mercedes down the bumpy road that led to a set of closed gates. What I saw on the other side, I could only describe as a compound. A few small buildings that resembled shacks sat next to a garage or warehouse. In the back, behind a large building, I could see trees along the shimmering water of a lake.

Then again, in this area, it could be a swamp. It was the large building in the center, with the members-only sign on the door, that I assumed was my target. It wasn't bad, I suppose, for a swamp rat. Clean white paint with a blue roof and red door.

My nose crinkled at the white van parked to the left. Why the hell would a bunch of bikers have a van. Wasn't that like sacrilege or something?

Whatever, I wasn't here for Chase's creep van. I tipped my head at the thick chain wrapped around the gates. A large lock on the other side glittered in the sunlight as if daring me to try and cross the forbidden barrier.

This was the best they had for security? Gotta say, I was a little disappointed. Weren't bikers supposed to be big, badass bastards?

"Some club you have here, Chase," I snorted and shifted into reverse.

I backed up, giving myself enough room to get some speed, and spun around to look out the windshield. Two men had come up to the gates and were standing there with their arms crossed. One tilted his head and narrowed his gaze as

I took a sip of my Perrier water. Almost as if fate was picking the music for my life, the loud chiming of bells rang through my speakers, 'Hells Bells.' Couldn't ask for a better song. The music started, and their eyes met mine as I revved the engine.

That's right motherfuckers, I'm coming in.

One shook his head while the other reached to his side. I popped the clutch, shifted, and slammed my foot on the gas. My tires spun, kicking up a cloud of dust as I shot forward and drove right through the gate, singing, "I won't take no prisoners."

The men acted quickly, throwing themselves off to the side to avoid the flung open gates. I yanked on the steering wheel, fishtailing my car to the left, and shot towards my target.

I kind of got why Ava did this stuff. The sound of rubber spinning out on gravel, along with the wind on my face, was exhilarating. I'd never felt so free and was a little disappointed when all hell didn't break loose.

Guess most of Chase's boys were in that mob I drove past because only a couple of guys came out from various places.

"You pricks better not shoot my car," I yelled as a few of them raised their pistols.

If there was one bullet hole in my car, I'd be taking it out of some-one's hide. Thankfully, no one pulled the trigger, and I was able to pull up to the large building in the center. They did follow me, though. Came right up to my Mercedes, surrounding me.

I snorted at their tense posture. What did they think I was going to do? Drive through their precious members-only building? It wasn't worth the paint it would cost to fix my car.

One of them slapped his hand down on my hood. "Get the fuck out of the car!"

"Do you mind?" I opened the door, stepped out onto the gravel, and nodded at his hand still pressed against my hood. "I just had it cleaned."

"What the fuck?" someone muttered, "Who invited Malibu Barbie?"

Ugh. Barbie, really?

I rolled my eyes. Was originality completely dead?

While the rest of them were gawking at me with either confusion or lust, one guy marched forward with his pistol raised.

"Who the fuck are you?"

I paused long enough to give him a quick scan. He was a big boy like the rest but couldn't be much older than me. There was a spark of youth and naivety in his turquoise eyes. Still, I had to admire him. He was more concerned with why I was here than checking out my ass.

"Get that gun out of my face," I snarled and spun around to open my back door.

He stepped forward, growling, "Look bitch..." but stopped when I pulled out the bouquet of flowers.

The furrow in his brow deepened when I threw my thumb at the building and asked, "Chase in there?"

One of the others answered. "You can't go in there."

My hand shot out, grabbing the nuts of the young one.

"Oh yeah," I gave enough of a squeeze for him to cry out and hunch over. "Who's going to stop me?"

The rest of them put their hands up in defeat, which I took as an invitation. I released his balls and smiled when his eyes rolled up to meet mine. He really wanted to hurt me, probably would if he wasn't in so much pain. Or, at least he'd try. I was Naomi Prescott. No one's victim.

I tapped him on the cheek and then headed for the red members-only door. "You should get some ice for that."

This dirty gravel wasn't doing my Jimmy Choo's any favors. I'd probably have to get rid of them after I left here. No big loss. They were last year's design. Normally, I'd have given them away by now, but they were the only ones that matched the olive coloring of my dress. Guess I'd have to do some shopping later.

"Shouldn't we stop her?" I heard one say.

"Fuck that, let Spider deal with his morning-after rejects."

I scoffed and threw the door open. Morning-after reject? Please, that would never happen. I was the one that did the rejecting. Besides, I would never sleep with someone named Spider. What the hell kind of juvenile crap was that?

When I stepped inside, I was a bit surprised. It was nicer than what I thought it would be. Not what I would consider nice, but it was okay.

It didn't look like a crack house with a mattress and dirt on the floor, which is what I expected. This place was clean and organized.

Road signs and various pictures hung on white walls that were accented by decent dark wooden floors. The stairs even had a rug going up them that was the same royal blue on their patches.

The color scheme was all over this place. Grey, black and blue, with just the right amount of red. Little highlights around picture frames and ornaments. A woman had to have decorated this place. No man could've done this.

Did they have women in motorcycle clubs? It would be kind of badass if they did. Some chick riding around with these big guys, holding her own. I might even like a girl like that, despite her lower social standing.

As I rounded the corner and headed for the second floor, I could hear voices wafting down the hallway.

"What the fuck were you thinking?" a deep tone growled.

That one kind of sounded like the really big guy from last night. The only reason I remembered him was because his size made him hard to miss.

I hadn't heard the next voice before. "You just declared war."

"My brother declared war eight years ago."

Now that one, I knew. Chase was apparently having a disagreement with his little friends. Well, he was about to have bigger problems.

After taking a minute to straighten my dress–one should always look their best–I strode down the hall. Whatever they were talking about came to a grinding halt when I threw open the door.

Four men–one of which was Chase–stood by a bar in a room that appeared to be some kind of lounge. A couple of couches sat on the right side, along with tables, chairs, and a pool table.

The left side housed a large bar and various other games, a dartboard and stuff like that. What threw me was the chess set in the corner. It was a nice one. A marble board with obsidian and quartz pieces, not something that should be here.

"Who the fuck let her in?"

My gaze swung over to Chase and the three men with him. Tanner I knew from back home, the other two I'd only seen once or twice.

"No one let me in."

"Get the fuck out, Princess." Chase's thick lips curled in a snarl. "You're not welcome here."

"Don't worry, I'll leave," I cocked my hip and gave him a sweet smile, "right after I thank you for your gift."

Chase shifted his gaze to the flowers in my hand, which was when I hurled it across the room.

"Fuck," he muttered and ducked out of the way as the vase soared through the air and smashed into the wall behind him.

Damnit, a little to the left, and I'd have hit him.

The guy with the darker complexion pushed off the bar, but Tanner pressed his hand to his chest and shook his head.

Whatever, let him come. I wasn't afraid of any of these pricks.

Chase's deep growl echoed through the air. "What the fuck is wrong with you?"

"What's wrong with me?" My palm flattened over my pounding heart. "You think flowers are going to fix a driveby. I got shot at, asshole!"

Something like guilt flashed across his face. Good! He should feel bad.

"I didn't tell those assholes to shoot up your sorority!"

"Really? That's the excuse you're going with?" I propped my hands on my hips. "Do me a favor, the next time you want to get someone killed, volunteer one of your friends. Mine are off-limits."

"Don't lie to me, Princess." Chase's dark eyes lit up as a smirk tugged at the corner of his mouth. "You don't have any friends."

This son of a bitch. He did not just say that to me. I balled my hands and took a deep breath.

Calm down, Naomi. He's not worth it. Proper girls control their temper.

"I think you hurt her feelings," Tanner snickered.

"The cunt doesn't have any feelings," Chase grumbled back.

Screw proper.

I snatched a cup off one the nearby tables and chucked it. Chase tried to move, but this time I got him. The mug hit him square in the chest. Satisfied, I smiled and spun around to leave.

"Get back here, you little bitch."

"Bite me," I sang over my shoulder and skipped down the stairs.

But he wasn't far behind. I'd made it down the first flight when my arm was seized, and I was pulled back into a wall of muscle.

Chase's warm breath warmed my skin as he growled in my ear. "You think you can come into my clubhouse and throw shit at me."

"Clubhouse," I scoffed. "What are you, four?"

Next thing I knew, I was spun around with my back slammed against the wall.

"You picked the wrong day to fuck with me, Princess."

"No, Chase," I spat out his name with disdain and disgust. "You picked the wrong girl to fuck with."

I shoved him back and lifted my knee, bring it up into his groin.

That's when everything changed.

In my experience, men had two reactions to getting kicked in the balls. They fell to the ground in a moaning heap, or they bent over, groaning in pain. Either way, it was enough to make them second guess their next action.

Chase didn't do either of those.

My knee connected with the most sensitive part of his body, and all I got in response was a discomfiting groan. That wasn't what scared me, though. It was the way his eyes darkened with rage and hatred.

I could see it pouring into him. Feel the anger radiating off him. I kicked him in the nuts, and all it did was piss him off!

Before I could make a run for it, his hand snapped up and wrapped around my neck.

"You think you're the first girl to kick me in the nuts?"

For the first time in my life, I didn't know what to do, so I slapped him. Hard. My palm flew through the air, striking his cheek and twisting his face to the side.

Take that asshole.

My heart dropped when he twisted his neck, and I was met with his glare. Chase's fingers twitched around my throat as he released a loud roar and punched the wall. His giant fist broke through the drywall beside my head, and all I could think was this was it.

I'd finally pushed someone past their resistance, and now I was going to die. I suppose there were worse things that could happen.

"Go ahead," I hissed. "Hit me."

He wouldn't be the first guy to hurt me. There was a reason I attached myself to Micha Kessler and his friends. No one with that kind of power was seen as vulnerable.

Chase's brows furrowed. "I'm not gonna hit you."

"Why not? You suddenly a good guy?"

"Make no mistake," he pressed in on me, "I'm far from fucking good."

I don't know why I was taunting him? The man was a good six inches taller than me and a massive wall of muscle. Christ sake, his forearm was as big as my thigh. The truly messed up part was that his hand around my neck wasn't stirring my sense of selfpreservation. It was turning me on.

The longer I stood there, staring at the dark scruff on his chiseled jaw, the more I wanted to run my fingers through his brown hair. I hated him with every fiber of my being, but goddammit, if a large part of me wasn't aching to reach down and grab his cock.

I decided to do something else instead.

Unlike my mother, I didn't slum it. And Chase Mathers might be able to withstand one hit to the nuts, but not two. Prepared to take him down, I lifted my leg.

Unfortunately, he was ready for that. His knee wedged between my thighs, clamping his legs around my leg before I could do anything.

"Not very smart, are you."

"Congratulations," I sang with an eye roll, "You managed to subdue a girl."

"Oh, Princess." He flattened his body up against mine and softly growled. "I haven't begun to subdue you yet."

I shifted, trying to get away from his knee. All that did was make me gasp as his leg pressed up against my core. My pulse picked up as his thigh flexed, tensing the solid muscle and adding more pressure.

"Shit," slipped through my lips before I could clamp my mouth shut.

It shouldn't be like this. My panties shouldn't be getting wet, and my body sure as hell shouldn't be soaking up his warmth. I'd only had two orgasms in my life, both of which I'd given myself, and neither of those felt as good as being over-powered by him did.

Chase's breath shallowed out as his gaze fell down to my hips. Any doubt I had about whether or not he could feel my arousal vanished when he lifted his leg and ground his thigh against me. My clit throbbed from the friction, shooting sparks of excitement up my spine.

"God, I hate you," I breathed and rocked my hips to feel it again.

"Don't worry, Princess." His hand left my neck and speared through my hair, roughly yanking my head to the side. "The feeling's mutual."

This was so not happening.

Gritting my teeth against the pleasure rolling through my body, I twisted my neck as much as I could and looked him right in the eyes. "Let me go."

"Not a fucking chance," he growled and grabbed my ass with his free hand, rolling my panty-clad mound along his strong thigh. "You're gonna come all over my leg."

"Good luck." I had a hard time getting myself off. Which was why I never blamed my lack of orgasm during sex on any of the four guys I'd been with.

My body simply wasn't built that way.

"You're halfway there already." His fingers dug in my ass, rocking my hips.

I moaned.

He groaned.

Fighting against the fog quickly filling my mind, I thought back to something he said to me the second time we met.

"Looks like I deserve your dick after all."

His jaw twitched. "You don't."

I reached down and palmed his already hard cock through his jeans while trying not to moan. He felt so big and thick that my pussy clenched with anticipation. But this wasn't about that. This was about winning and losing.

And I. Didn't. Lose.

Gotcha asshole.

I curled my hand around the back of his neck and pulled him in so I could whisper in his ear. "I think your dick disagrees."

That's right, prick. I'm better at this game than you.

I was wrong.

"That's the difference between a boy and a man." He leaned in, bringing his mouth a breath away from mine. "My dick doesn't run the show."

His mouth crashed down on mine before I could take a breath. And my God, was he ever a man. Soft, thick lips moved against mine so expertly that I didn't realize I'd opened my mouth until his tongue swept over mine.

I shouldn't like the taste of his cheap toothpaste or how his masculine scent poured through me, but I couldn't help it.

One growl in my mouth was all it took to make me stop trying to pull away. The deep grumble rolled through me, washing away my resistance. I moaned and wrapped my arms around him, melting into his solid form.

Something in the back of my brain told me this was wrong, and for a brief second, I tried to fight it. Pulling on his hair and biting his lip, Chase returned my actions, digging his teeth into my lip as he yanked my head back.

I'm not sure how my legs wound up wrapped around his waist or when he started to palm my breast.

One thing I did know, I'd never been happier to hear Tanner's voice in my life.

"Oh shit, my bad."

Our make-out session ended faster than if a bucket of ice water was tossed on us. We both stopped and slowly turned to see a smiling Tanner.

He held up his hands, "Didn't mean to interrupt."

Chase dropped me and stepped back. "Get the fuck out of my clubhouse."

I straightened my dress, lifted my chin, and snarled, "Stay the fuck off my campus," before strutted out.

Chapter 7

CHASE

My fists balled, tightening the skin around my scrapped knuckles and sending a dull ache crawling up my arm. Driving my fist through the wall scratched them all to hell. Probably didn't help when I beat on the Reaper we had tied up in the basement.

Or, I should say, formerly had. Tanner was currently out, feeding the gators with what was left of his corpse. There were bonuses to living near a swamp.

I hadn't planned on killing my brother's man. Not until I'd gotten information out of him, but I was so pissed off at that little bitch, I had to take it out on someone. And Tanner wasn't up for a round of eat-my-fist, so I paid our prisoner a visit.

Fucking Naomi Prescott. Who the hell did she think she was? Marching in here like she owned the place, with her *I think your dick disagrees.* Trying to bait me. Nice try, Princess.

I dropped that high school shit when I was twelve. I should've tanned her ass. She seemed to like that shit. I know I did. The bitch had a fantastic ass. The way it bounced when my belt smacked off her skin…

"Fuuuck," I groaned while pushing on Grace's head, driving my cock down her throat.

Did I feel bad for treating her like a human fleshlight? No. Grace chose to be a sweet butt. She wanted to get used. Their whole purpose was to please patched members. Except, she wasn't pleasing me. Nothing to do on her end.

The chick had a mouth like a hoover. Someone else was occupying my mind. And trust me I was trying to rid myself of her snarky fucking smile, but every time I licked my lips, I could taste her on the tip of my tongue. It was more refreshing than cold Corona and lime.

"Goddammit," I yelled, slammed my fist on my desk. "This shit isn't working."

Grace popped my dick out of her mouth and fluttered her light eyes up at me.

"Is it that girl that was here earlier? She seemed kind of young."

She was young. Too fucking young. Naomi was only a year older than Riley. Which basically made me the perverted uncle type I told her to stay away from.

"Would it help if I called you an asshole?" Grace's lips tipped down in a fake frown. "I could throw something at you."

My face dropped. I was gonna punch Tanner the next time I saw him.

"Did I tell you to stop sucking my dick?"

One brow arch was all it took for Grace to slurp my cock back in her mouth.

As if divine intervention heard my thoughts, Tanner burst in my office.

"Hey, Boss."

Welcome to next time, asshole.

"Come here," I waved him over.

The grinning idiot strutted right up. The second he was within reach, I swung my arm across the desk and slapped him.

He stumbled back into the chair behind him, rubbing his cheek. "Ouch."

"Stop telling the whole damn club my business."

"But is it still your business when you're making out with it on the stairs?"

I sighed and dropped my head in my hand. Yeah, I probably shouldn't have done that.

"How'd it go?" I asked, seeking a change in subject.

He propped his muddy boot up on my desk and gave me a big smile. "The gators ate well today."

"Wilder give you any problems?"

"Nah," he shook his head. "He was busy doing his own thing."

Grace instantly popped up from under the desk with wide eyes. "Is Wilder here?"

"Shut the fuck up," I growled and pushed her back down.

Wilder had a way of making people uneasy. He was one of the few that sent a chill up my spine. Even Preston Whitley didn't do that, and that kid was one cold son of a bitch. His stare was hard and empty, but Wilder's was completely lifeless.

Difference between a sociopath and a psychopath, I suppose, and I was pretty damn sure Wilder was a psychopath. Of course, his choice to live in the run-down amusement park didn't help any. Fucking creepy-ass clowns everywhere. I shivered just thinking about it.

"I hate to interrupt," Tanner tipped his chin at my desk, "but Micha Kessler is outside."

My brow arched. "Micha Kessler?"

"Yup."

My first thought was that something had happened to Riley, but if that was the case, it'd be more likely I'd get a call.

"What the fuck does he want?"

This wasn't exactly the type of place any Kessler would hang out. Well, except for Mason. Micha's brother was fucking idiot. I could see him waltzing in here, thinking he was just one of the guys.

Tanner shrugged. "Says he wants to talk to you."

What the hell did that prick want to talk to me about? This better not be more of their Order of Ravens and Wolves bullshit. I told his old man I wasn't interested in joining their rich boy club.

"You want me to tell him to piss off?"

I briefly considered letting him shoot the asshole fucking my niece, then I'd have Riley all up in my business. And no one wanted that. She might be a tiny thing, but she sure could pack a punch.

I bet she could take down half the guys in here before they realized what was happening. I fucking loved that girl.

"No," I sighed and stood up, tucking dick away, "I'll go see what he wants."

Anything was better than the mind-numbing blow job I was pretending to enjoy. Besides, Tanner probably took my place the second I left.

I nodded at a couple of prospects I passed on the stairs. Since my outburst yesterday, everyone had been walking on eggshells. Rooms quieted down, guys whispered, and three prospects decided this wasn't the life for them.

Beast tried to give me shit about it until I pointed out that it was better to weed out the cowards now than in the middle of a gunfight.

If they were looking for a place to party and get pussy every night, they could join a frat. We weren't the nice guys that ran off dealers and took guns off the street. We put them there.

Our world was dark and dangerous. There'd always be some motherfucker who wanted what was ours, or a war waiting to be fought. I didn't have time to hold their hands.

The only way we'd survive was if every patch-wearing member was ready to lay his life down for their brother. Unity was the one thing my brother didn't have. I might expect a lot, but if anyone of them needed backup, my hog would be the first to fire up.

That was why I knew we'd win. Fear didn't buy the same kind of loyalty that respect did. And, I got my three Reaper heads, plus one more.

I walked out into the warm afternoon sun and marched across the grounds. Micha Kessler was leaning back against a shiny black Jeep, his arms crossed and a bored expression on his face. I propped my hip against the gate and watched the crowd gathered around him.

"That's a nice cage you have," one of my boys said while planting his ass on the hood of Micha's Jeep. And not nicely either. The metal groaned as he dropped his ass hard. "Daddy buy it for you?"

Snake, the newest member to earn his diamond one percent patch, stalked around Micha and dragged his key across the shiny black paint. Even I cringed at the screeching sound ringing through the air.

"Looks like Richie Rich needs a new paint job." Snake was a big boy who had a rough life. A few of his foster parents were well off and let's just say, he wasn't particularly fond of people with money.

I had to hand it to Micha, though. He was surrounded by a bunch of growly assholes who'd like nothing more than to eat that expensive watch around his wrist, and he didn't even flinch. Not even when Snake reached out and snatched the sunglasses off his face.

"Thanks, Richie Rich," Snake tapped the side of Micha's face, "I needed a new pair."

Micha huffed out a sigh and shrugged. "Who am I to argue if you want my leftovers."

Ah fuck, I had to stop this shit now. Three of those Reaper heads I got last night were taken by Snake.

"Don't you guys have somewhere else to be?" I said, pushing off the fence to head over before my niece's boyfriend ended up with a knife in his gut.

A few of the boys gave a disgruntled mutter, but they all quickly dispersed. Snake was the only one who paused long enough to glare back at Micha. Can't say I blamed him. I didn't like the guy either.

The fact that Micha was the spitting image of his father wasn't winning him any points. Three days in Ashen Springs was all it took for the Kesslers to pop up on my radar. It didn't matter how much a man dressed up or what kind of face he wore out in public. A criminal was still a criminal, and Louis Kessler was one of the shadiest mother-fuckers I knew.

Micha tilted his head towards the group, walking away. "Enjoy that?"

"A little."

"You look good." His dark eyes rolled over me, stopping on the cigarette behind my ear. "When did you take up smoking?"

Not in the mood for small talk, I sighed, "What do you want, Micha?"

"So, right down to business then?"

I didn't say anything. Despite what connection he thought I had to his group of thugs, we weren't friends.

"Okay," this time, it was him who sighed, "I heard about what happened on campus the other night."

That's what this was about. Derek already gave me shit for that, and I gave even less fucks what Micha thought.

"So?"

"So," he said, "I have some information that could help."

"Yeah, sure." I barked out a laugh. Micha was a boy playing man. His balls had barely dropped. How the fuck was he going to help me? "Take your detention slips and go home."

"What's your problem, Chase. My age?" Micha pushed off the Jeep and straightened up. "Or my name?"

I may not be a fan of his old man, but that was beside the point. "Do you have any idea what your stepping into?"

"I've fought a few wars in my time."

"See," I tsked, "I don't think you understand. This isn't one of your schoolyard tiffs. It's a full-out war. Death has come to Miami, and he doesn't give a shit who gets away. When this is over, the streets will be paved in blood. The only important thing is who's blood it is. Ours, or theirs. That's not something you can pay people to forget."

"What if you could win it without civilian casualties?"

"That's a nice idea." I crossed my arms, "but it's a big city. Lots of people to get in the way."

Micha's brow rose. "Riley said you're a fan of chess."

"Riley talks too much."

I wouldn't say I was a fan of the game, so much as pushed into learning it. Puberty hit me like a ton of bricks. Until then, I was a scrawny kid. Chess club seemed like the thing to do in school.

"You should know that sometimes the best piece on the board," he reached into his jacket and pulled out a large manila envelope, "is the pawn."

"What's that?"

"The key to taking your brother down."

Why should I believe anything he said? My eyes narrowed on the envelope in his hand. Fuck it. What did I have to lose? I snatched the envelope, and Micha sat back while I went through the contents. Most of it was bank statements and docking slips.

I was about to throw the papers back at him when I flipped to a newspaper article. It wasn't the story that caught my attention. It was the picture. Ashen Springs mayor christening a boat called the Aurora.

The same boat was on the docking information. And in the background was a man with dark hair and a large red Reaper patch.

"Jax," I growled, instantly recognizing the scar on my brother's left cheek. It was one of the last things I gave him.

"We traced all the mayor's deposits back to an account in the Cayman Islands under the name Ian Mathers. Sound familiar?"

My eyes rolled up. It should sound familiar. That was my father's name. It was possible that my old man had a stash of money none of us knew about.

"When was it opened?"

"Seven years ago."

That was two years after he died.

I glared down at the picture of Ashen Springs' Mayor. If I didn't hate the fucker before, I sure as hell did now. "What's my brother paying him for?"

"Don't know. He hid that well," Micha tipped his head and squinted against the sun, "but whatever it is, it has to do with that boat."

While I was appreciative of the information, there was something I didn't get.

"Why are you doing this?"

"You're the last of the wolves."

I grumbled. Not this shit again.

"Like it or not, you're one of us, Chase, and we help our own. Just like you'd help anyone of them," he added, nodding his head at the bikers watching us.

Apparently, Tanner finished with Grace because he was propped up against the clubhouse with his ankles crossed and eyes trained on us. Neither one of us trusted Louis Kessler or his son. Though a lot of that might have to do with how he took Riley.

I thought about taking out Micha and his thugs so many times, but if Riley wanted me involved, she would've asked for help. Unfortunately, I couldn't control who she fell in love with, that didn't mean I had to like it.

"Tell your old man I'm not interested…" Information like this wasn't given for free.

"My father has nothing to do with this."

I believed that about as much as I believed Naomi was really a sweet person deep down. Micha was Louis Kessler's perfect little protégé.

"Go home, Micha," I sighed and turned to leave.

"People are always comparing me to my father. Expecting me to do what he would do or make the same choices he would."

I stopped and fisted my hands.

"I would think you'd understand that."

Oh, I understood it. All too well.

"What do you expect me to do? Roll into town and execute your mayor?" I glanced back at him, "Find someone else to take care of your problem."

"Sure, you could go for Clive himself, but you won't find out shit about your brother," Micha pointed out.

He was right. The second Jax thought I was onto him, he'd cut his loss. My best chance at catching him off guard was to by convincing Clive Prescott to cooperate.

"It's a good idea," I'd give the kid that much, "but you don't know my brother. Clive won't cross him. It'd be bad for everyone he loved if he did."

"There's one thing my father says that I agree with. He who holds the most leverage has all the power." Micha tipped his head at the file in my hand. "Our mayor has one weakness, and she happens to be going to school in your city."

I glanced down at the blonde little girl in the picture holding the mayor's hand. Fucking Naomi. Making daddy's little princess serve me until her old man broke? Now that was a plan I would thoroughly enjoy.

I looked Micha right in the eyes so he'd understand how serious I was. "You understand what I'll do to her?"

"I guess daddy better cooperate then," he shrugged.

I shook my head. My niece's boyfriend really was a cold bastard. I could at least respect that.

Turning my head, I whistled at Tanner, who was waiting for me to call him over.

His gaze shifted to Micha as he walked over. "What's up?"

"Message Clive Prescott," I slapped the stack of papers off Tanner's chest, "Tell him he has until ten o'clock tonight to tell us everything we want to know about his deal with my brother."

"Or what," he asked, with an arched brow.

"Or I'll take his little princess as payment."

Daddy better come through, or Naomi would find out exactly how much I fucking hated her.

Chapter 8

NAOMI

I glanced at the Gucci watch my father gave me for Christmas. Was it only ten-thirty? Ugh, this was the worst date ever.

"Coach said he had the best time on the team."

My brow cocked as my date's chest puffed out with pride. Why did I agree to this? The guy was cute, light hair and dark eyes. The designer jeans and red polo shirt he was wearing told me he had some style.

His downfall was the mind-numbing boredom of constant sports talk. What was it with football players?

"I tackled that prick faster than…"

With a sigh, I looked down at my hand. I'd had this French manicure for almost a week now. Maybe Yui was still up? Booking a manicure would kill five minutes. This time, I might go with a more vibrant color, like blue or green.

It would narrow down my outfit choices, but I could always go shopping for that, and there was the cutest little purse I had my eye on.

My date's hand skimmed down my back. "That dress looks great on you."

Of course, it did.

"Thanks," I grumbled and drained the last of the beer from my red solo cup. "You don't look so bad yourself…"

Fuck… what was his name? Tim? Tom?

He leaned in and waggled his eyebrows. "I bet you'd look even better on my bed."

That was the best pickup line he could come up with? Seriously? Guess I shouldn't expect too much. His idea of a good date wasn't going out for dinner or to a movie.

No, this idiot took me to a frat party. Instead of enjoying a nice crème brulee, I was trapped in a stinky house full of drunk boys and horny girls.

"What do you say, Sweet Thing?" My date wrapped his arm around my waist and pulled me into him.

I hummed and cocked my head at the Alpha Theta Sigma paddle hanging on the wall. The handle wasn't propped up properly. One hard bang and that thing was coming down on someone's head.

"You wanna test my bed theory?"

My gaze shifted from his attempt at a charming smile to the group gathered by the stairs. They were all carefree, talking and laughing. Did they not see the paddle? And don't even get me started on the guy with a rat tail.

Tim or Tom ran his nose up my neck. "I bet I could show you a better time than any of those small-town boys you're used to."

I highly doubted that.

Why was no one doing anything about that paddle? Oh, for Christ's sake. Did I have to do everything myself?

I shrugged out of my date's embrace, snatched a pair of scissors off the counter, and strutted over to the group.

Using the scissors, I carefully push the paddle into a more secure spot, because I wasn't touching that thing. After which, I spun around, looked at the guy with the rat tail, and quickly snipped it off.

"No," I said, slapping the braided lock of hair and scissors in his palm. "There's no excuse for this shit."

His mouth opened with unspoken words as I walked back to my date, who looked just as shocked as the other guy.

"You were saying?"

"Uh, right." He shook the shock off his face and smiled. "Do you wanna–"

I pressed my finger to his lips, cutting him off.

Bailey, my Mayberry roommate, was slumped over the couch across the room, clearly drunk. Not particularly out of place. This was a party, after all.

Half of the sorority was stumbling around this place. My problem came from the punk Bailey was giggling at and the way he kept checking out her ass.

"Another paddle catch your eye?" My date tipped his head, "because I've got one in my room."

Oh God, this idiot was going to make me throw up.

"Hold that thought," I muttered and left.

I could deal with whatever his name was later. Hey, maybe I'd luck out, and he'd find someone else to hit on?

Thankfully all those high school parties prepared me for elegantly making my way through a crowd of drunken morons. Some I pushed out of the way, while others I simply stepped over.

Of course, there was always that one person who thought I was their best friend and hung off me like a cheap suit. Not too hard to get rid of. It was just a matter of redirecting her to someone else. In this case, a strapping young football player who was just as inebriated as she was.

By the time I reached the green couch Bailey was sprawled across, I was more than ready for this night to end.

"Come on, Bailey," I grabbed her arm and pulled her up, "It's time to go."

The guy she was giggling with apparently didn't like me interrupting them because he stood up and rolled his shoulders back.

"I got her," he lifted his hand to touch her face. "We were having fun, weren't we, Hailey?"

I slapped his hand away. "Her name is Bailey."

The guy was clearly a rapist. How hard was it to remember a name?

This prick was going to give me a hard time. I could tell by the way his jaw ticked.

Bailey broke the tension by giggling and flopping her head back on my chest. "Q is cute."

Q? Really?

"No, he's not," I grumbled and hoisted her up. At least she was small. There was no way I could hold someone my height up in these shoes. "You're drunk."

Bailey pouted, "But I only had one drink."

"Is that so?" My eyes narrowed on Q's stupid smirk. *I fucking knew it.* "Ava!"

A few seconds later, my friend came busting out of a back room. Her blonde hair was sticking out through the face grill of a football helmet, and a pair of shoulder pads were draped over her shoulders. I didn't want to know where her pants were or how she got the pink tutu.

"Bailey's drunk," I said as she came running up.

"You want me to take her home?"

I cocked a brow down at Ava's almost five-foot frame. "How are *you* going to take her home?"

Ava cocked her hip and took a minute to size up Bailey before she jumped up, clapped her hands, and ran off with a squeal.

Well, that was super helpful.

"I can take her home."

My gaze snapped back over to the prick that drugged my roommate.

"Listen, Q," I snarled while poking my finger in his chest, "go find some other girl to rape, this one's mine."

She wasn't mine, mine. Other than a couple of threesomes I'd had with Logan, I had no interest in riding down that train. When I said Bailey was mine, I meant one of my girls.

Yeah, she was small town and had shit for fashion sense–she was still sporting pigtails for Christ's sake–but she was in the same sorority. Lord knows how she got there, but there she was, which made her a 'sister' as the housemother called it, and therefore mine.

I sure as hell wasn't going to let some jock douchebag steal her virginity because she was too naive to know better than to take a drink from a stranger.

Q's jaw dropped. "I wasn't going to–"

"Run along, little boy," I waved my hand, dismissing him.

He muttered a few choice words but promptly left. A short time after, Ava came back pushing a friggin wheel-barrel.

"Okay, I got it."

I glanced down at the red bucket. "A wheel-barrel?"

"Yup," Ava nodded.

"You're going to push her home in a wheel-barrel?"

Her grey eyes sparkled as her nose scrunched up at me. "Uh, yeah?"

She seemed almost insulted that I would question this logic because taking someone home in a wheel-barrel was apparently a normal everyday thing in her mind right now.

Tomorrow, she might be building a go-cart out of milk cartons? Funny thing is, I guarantee that go-cart would not only work but would kick every other cart's ass. So, I shrugged and dropped Bailey's deadweight in the trough.

Whatever. I wouldn't have to carry her, so it worked for me. Besides, Ava seemed to be having fun. She ran through the house, making siren sounds. Which I assumed she'd continue to do until they got home.

Though, I was kind of curious how she planned on getting Bailey up the stairs. I might've even went with them if my date hadn't come over.

"You want to get out of here?"

God yes.

"I can walk you home?"

Ugh, he had to come.

I sighed, "Alright, let's go."

It took a few minutes to get through the crowd and exit the house, but I felt a little relieved the second we stepped out into the night air. Not completely. I mean, Tom was still here, so...

Tim slung his arm over my shoulder, and I pretended to listen to his jabbering as we strolled down the sidewalk. Other than the music coming from his frat house, the campus was fairly quiet.

The harmony of a soft breeze mingling with our footsteps reminded me of home. The way Ashen Springs stilled under the moonlight filled me with a sense of serenity.

That peaceful feeling was different here. I still got the graceful sway of plant life moving in the dark, and the moon still cast a glow over the ground, but it wasn't still. I suppose no city this size was.

There was always someone out and about or cars driving down the street. It was that active life that made me appreciate moments like this more. Times, when for just a few minutes, the world stopped, and I could hear myself breathe.

This moment was destroyed by a single sound. A growl rumbled through the air, slicing through my ears as a Harley rolled past. My gaze locked on the face of the driver, who smirked at me and shot down the road. What the hell was Tanner doing here?

Was Chase with him?

Tim stopped and eyed Tanner's retreading form. "Maybe we should go back?"

Everyone on campus knew about what happened. Sororities weren't typically shot at, so it was kind of big news. Some people thought it was exciting. Others speculated that one of us was in the mob or something.

Then, there were the people who avoided the house because they were scared. Apparently, my date was the latter.

"You'll be fine," I said and tugged him down the sidewalk.

We made it two steps before he pulled away.

"I should go. I have to get up early for practice and…"

I rolled my eyes. "Whatever."

That was all he needed to hear. Tom took off yelling, "I'll call you," over his shoulder.

"Please don't," I grumbled and continued on my way home.

When I walked into the Pi Kappa house, I was greeted by grunts and groans. At first, I thought one of the girls was getting it on in the sitting room. Last week, Cammie had a guy over, and we all saw more than we cared to. The sound wasn't coming from there, though.

It was coming from the stairs, where Ava – still dressed in her football/ballerina attire – was tugging on a sheet. At the other end, wrapped up in the red cloth, was a passed-out Bailey.

"What are you doing?"

"I'm taking her to bed." Ava planted her feet on the step and pulled with all her might.

Her face strained with the effort it took her to drag Bailey up one step.

I let out a breath and pinched the bridge of my nose. "Why didn't you just put her on the couch?"

Ava stopped mid-tug and furrowed her brows at a doorway to the left, where a pillowy couch could be seen.

"Huh? That'd probably be easier."

"Yeah," I nodded. "Here, I'll help you."

I moved to scoop up Bailey, but Ava jumped down the stairs and pushed me away.

"I can do it."

"Ava…"

"I can," she wrapped the sheet around her waist and stormed across the hall, dragging Bailey behind her. "See?"

I'd met a few girls with a Napoleon complex. Micha's girlfriend Riley, being one of the most predominant, but she didn't have shit on Ava. I could ignore her and put Bailey on the couch myself.

That wouldn't solve anything because Ava would push her off, roll her back to the bottom of the stairs and do it herself. When she got an idea in her head, no one, and I mean no one was going to convince her otherwise. Which, in this case, appeared to be the continuing care of Bailey.

"Fine," I waved my hand and walked up the stairs.

It'd be nice to have the room to myself anyways. Bailey's patchwork quilt and little handmade trinkets were a strain on my eyes. I wasn't used to sharing my space. A large part of me suspected that Ava housed us together on purpose. It, sure as hell, wasn't for Bailey's benefit.

I was not what some considered nice. If someone looked fat in their pants, I was going to tell them. We'd been here for two weeks now, and I'd made my Mayberry roommate cry seven times.

Not that I was keeping score, but she had run away sobbing more times than Cammie, and that girl was an utter moron. Bringing some redneck, piece-of-trash in the house. What was she thinking?

I stripped off my dress, slipped into a teddy, and crawled into bed.

I could understand Cammie's choice if the guy was at least good-looking. Nice firm muscles and strong hands that could really dig into a girl's ass. The kind of guy that could hold her up against the wall and just take what he wanted, that I could understand.

Maybe a couple tattoos and a little bit of facial hair. Not too much, though, just enough that it would scratch her skin when he kissed her.

Someone like Chase. Yes, the man was a brute and utterly insufferable, but he was okay to look at. All hard, and demanding, and big.

My breath picked up as my hands danced across my stomach.

Holy crap, was he big. Not the kind of big that would scare a girl off. He was the kind that would stretch her open and fill her up completely.

'That's the difference between a boy and a man.'

I slipped my hand under my lace thong and slid my finger through my folds. Spreading them open like I imagined he would do.

Chapter 9

CHASE

My arms braced on my handlebars and leaned forward as Naomi skittered across the street, heels clicking on the asphalt. I watched the moonlight bounce off her golden hair that flowed like a waterfall down her back to that perfect ass tightly wrapped in black fabric.

Was she wearing a tiny little thong under that dress, or was she secretly a granny panties kind of girl? I couldn't wait to find out.

"There she is." Mannix bumped me with his elbow. "Let's go."

I held up my hand. "Not yet."

Every muscle in my body was ready to ride over there and grab her now, but this shit had to go down a certain way. Naomi wasn't the kind of girl to just fall in line. I'd have to break the bitch down.

Something I was very much looking forward to doing. Clive Prescott pretty much told us to go to hell, which is exactly where I planned on dragging his daughter.

The prick may as well have handed his daughter over on a silver fucking platter. Every carnal desire that cunt made me feel was going to be taken out on that tight body of hers.

By the time I was done with that little bitch, she wouldn't be daddy's good girl anymore. She'd be mine.

"What are we waiting for?" Mannix whined, "She's alone. There's no one out. We couldn't ask for better timing."

I glared over at him and reiterated, "Not yet."

"You're making this more difficult than it has to be," he sighed and crossed his arms.

"Calm down." Tanner slapped him on the back. "You can't rush this shit."

"It's a kidnapping." Mannix rolled his glare Tanner's way. "Rushing is kind of in the job description."

Tanner let out an exasperated breath.

"You see that?" He said, pointing through the bushes we were hiding behind at Naomi as she slipped into her sorority house. "That's what we call an alpha female. Very hard to tame. You can't just rush out and grab the bitch. You have to make a show of it. Charge into her pack and let everyone know who's in charge."

I was a little concerned that Tanner's fucked up safari explanation actually made sense.

Mannix just snorted. "Okay, Davy Crockett."

While we both arched a brow at him, Tanner was the one to question it.

"Davy Crockett?"

"Yeah motherfucker, Davy Crockett," Mannix ground out at him. "You got a problem with Davy Crockett?"

"No, man. I ain't got no problem." Tanner held up his hands in defeat and shook his head, but I could see the smile tugging on the corner of his mouth. "Davy's a cool dude. He's got that raccoon hat and shit."

Mannix grumbled under his breath and shifted his gaze back to the house. Thank-fucking God. I did not want another snow-cones-are-made-from-real-snow incident. I'd just fished Tanner's scrawny ass out of some alley and brought him back to the clubhouse.

The first thing he did was get in a three-hour-long argument with Mannix. After which, he proceeded to annoy the shit out of Beast. I was honestly surprised the idiot survived puberty.

"How fucking long are we gonna wait?"

"Oh, relax," Tanner snickered, "raccoons are nocturnal. There's plenty of hunting left to do."

Mannix's unimpressed glare turned my way. "I'm gonna shoot him."

"Careful, motherfucker. You may have fought at the Alamo, but I'm the quickest draw in the west." Tanner pulled out his 9mm and spun it around his finger.

Mannix clicked his tongue off his cheek and arched an impatient eyebrow my way.

Honestly, I didn't know what I was waiting for. We could've grabbed Naomi when she came out of that party down the street, but the only thing I could focus on was the yuppie prick with his arm around her shoulder.

I was so close to shooting that son of a bitch, that I had to send Tanner to drive by and scare him off. Which I knew would work because of the looks we got when we rolled onto campus. Guess the Reaper drive-by was good for something.

I fired up the engine and kicked my hog into gear. "Let's do this."

Tanner and Mannix straightened up and followed my lead. Our engines roared through the silence as we drove across the street and onto the bullet riddle yard. Despite what some thought, I did feel bad about that. It was never my intention to put those girls in danger. Naomi... well that was different.

Tanner and I stepped off our hogs and took the few steps to the door while Mannix stayed with the bikes to keep watch. The last thing I expected to see when we walked inside, was that crazy little blonde struggling to lift an unconscious girl on the couch.

The act itself wasn't out of the ordinary. The tiny thing had her feet propped up against the coffee table and was using her back to push the other girl up. It was the outfit she was wearing.

We stopped and looked at her.

She stopped and looked at us.

Tanner propped his elbow on my shoulder. "Aww, isn't she cute?"

Cute is definitely not the word I'd use. I cocked a brow at the way too big shoulder pad and pink tutu the girl was wearing.

"You want some help, Sweetheart?"

She glared at Tanner through the helmet on her head. "I can do it."

"Well, you have fun with that," I slapped Tanner on the back and then threw my thumb over my shoulder. "Naomi upstairs?"

"Yup," Preston's sister nodded and spun around to use her arms to roll the other girl up on the couch. "Her room's the one with the prom queen sash."

Of course, it was.

I left Tanner to deal with her and headed up the stairs. One good thing about crazy, most times, they didn't give a shit what you were doing.

Sure enough, once I rounded the corner at the top of the stairs, there it was. A white sash hanging across a door down the hall. I stepped up and fingered the Ashworth emblem beside the words prom queen. Was this scrap of fabric really that important to Naomi?

This title didn't mean shit in the real world. Half the prom queens I knew were now flipping burgers or sucking dick for a living. It pissed me off that she put this much stock in something so stupid.

Time to show the prom queen what her future holds.

I flung open the door and froze.

Various tiaras and way too many clothes took up half of the room, but I was more focused on the bed. Naomi's head was back, eyes closed as her lips parted with quiet moans.

I licked my lips and slid my gaze over her heaving chest to the hand I could see moving beneath the pink silk sheet.

Fuck me.

"Damn. We have good timing."

Naomi squealed, and I twisted my neck to glare at Tanner's stupid smile.

There was no hesitation. I growled, "Get the fuck out," and shoved him in the hall.

After that, I kicked the door shut and spun around. Naomi didn't freak out or try to cover herself up. She simply sat up and stared at me with hatred burning in those light green eyes. I could literally feel the heat of her rage burning through the air.

"Enjoy the show?"

"Not as much as you." My eyes landed on her pert nipples, pressing against the thin fabric of her white teddy. "Did you come, Princess?"

"That wasn't going to happen," her pink lips twisted in a sneer, "I was thinking about you."

My dick twitched.

Yeah, you fucking were.

She arched a perfectly shaped brow as if daring me to challenge her. I held back the smirk tugging at the corner of my mouth and leaned against the small dresser next to the door.

Alright, Princess, I'll play your game.

"Well, by all means, continue," I waved my hand and crossed my ankles. "I've never been one to deny a lady her orgasm."

"You wanna watch me?"

I damn near blew my load when she tore the sheet off her body and spread her legs. She was a thong kind of girl. The one she was wearing didn't have much for coverage either.

I could see her juicy pink pussy right through that scrap of white lace. Almost fucking groaned at the sight, and then her fingers slid underneath.

"Fucking pervert." Her finger twirled around her clit, making her mouth part in a gasp. "You like that?"

Fuck yeah, I did.

I could watch this shit all day. It was incredibly hard to stop myself from whipping my cock out and joining her. Especially when she dipped her finger inside her opening.

My cock got harder with every flick and swirl. Until I noticed something. When I looked up into her eyes, I didn't see lust or need. I saw frustration. Ashworth's perfect prom queen had no idea how to get herself off.

Now, this was interesting.

"How's it going, Princess? That pussy ready to pop yet?"

"Of course not," her jaw ticked, "you're here."

I pushed off the dresser and stalked over to her, taking my time to enjoy the moment. The smell of Naomi's wet cunt, along with tiny little huffs of irritation. It was so fucking erotic. I couldn't stop myself from crawling over her.

"I'm never going to come if you're this close," she breathed up at me.

"Is that the problem?" I tipped my head to roll my eyes down her curves. "Or is it because you have no idea what you're doing?"

"Of course, I know what I'm doing." She stopped fingering herself and glared up at me. "It's my body."

A slow smirk spread across my face. "I don't think you do."

That pissed her off. Her hand snapped out of her panties and swung at me. I snatched her wrist and sucked her fingers in my mouth, groaning as the sweet taste of her pussy exploded across my tongue. She tasted just as fucking good as she looked.

"Is this your idea of foreplay?" she snarled, trying to sound pissed, but I saw her shiver. "Cause it's seriously lacking."

My tongue wrapped around her fingers, sucking off every drop, before I slid them out of my mouth and slammed her arm down on the bed above her head.

"Foreplay would imply that I was going to fuck you." I tsked and pulled her other arm up. "Let's call this a lesson." I leaned down and growled in her ear, "You have to earn my dick, Princess."

"I don't want your dick."

Ignoring her snarls, I slid my hand down her stomach and over her hip to the scrap of lace nestled between her thighs.

"The pussy is a delicate creature," I traced my fingers along the edge of her thong and up her wet slit. "Sometimes, you have to coax her into cooperating."

Naomi shuttered out a breath and lifted her hips. "You can't coax shit."

"The clit for example," I continued, "is so sensitive, sometimes you just need to add a little friction." She gasped as I pressed down on her panties and swirled around her clit. "Lace is the perfect material to give a little bit of texture to the feeling. With the right amount of pressure…"

I pinched her swollen nub between my thumb and forefinger, attempting to pull a moan from her. Those pouty pink lips parted and sucked in a breath, but no sound came out.

That wasn't going to deter me. Before we left this room, I'd not only get my moan. I'd hear her scream.

"Of course, there's always the stubborn pussies."

One flick of my wrist, I had her thong torn off and flung across the room. Her tight walls clamped around my fingers as I shoved them in her wet entrance, causing a deep groan to rumbled through my chest.

She was so fucking hot and silky that it took all my willpower to tame my aching cock.

"Those ones you have to go deep for," I said while hooking my fingers to look for that spot that made women's eyes cross. "Drag the orgasm out kicking and screaming."

The instant I felt that spongy flesh, I went for it, pounding my fingers into her hard. Banging that spot over and over again.

Finally, she gave me what I wanted. Naomi's back arch as her mouth spewed out cursed moans.

"Feel that, Princess," I slid my tongue up her neck, savoring the salty taste of her sweat-coated ecstasy. "That's a man controlling your pussy."

Three more pumps and her nails were digging into my shoulders as she screamed out an orgasm that squirted all over my hand.

There was nothing more beautiful than a woman cumming. Naomi took that to a whole new level. Her entire body flushed as her eyes rolled in the back of her head, and I'd never wanted anyone more.

I couldn't stop myself from grabbing a hold of her hair and slamming her head back.

"You're gonna fucking do that again," I growled and fucked her harder with my fingers.

Even though she shook her head, I got what I wanted. Orgasms were easy once the g-spot was triggered. A few good strokes, and she was going off again, this time, begging me not to do it again.

"No more," she pled through the shudders rocking her system. "I can't."

As much as I'd love to keep this up all night and put the bitch in her place, I came here for a reason. There'd be plenty of time to fuck with her later.

"Get dressed," I said, giving her pussy a good slap. "You're coming with me."

Chapter 10

NAOMI

"I'm not going anywhere with you."

My palms flattened on Chase's broad chest. Partially to stop the room from spinning, but mostly to push him off me. Neither of which worked.

His brow lifted, "You seem to think you have a choice."

I don't care to what voodoo God he prayed to make me come, no one told me what to do. He just got lucky, that's all. I'd worked myself up before he got here, and it was my body, so one could argue that I gave myself an orgasm.

"Unless you think you'll have a hard time walking?"

My eyes rolled at his statement. This time when I pushed him, he rolled off me. I shrugged off the shiver racing across my skin and sang, "Feel free to leave anytime."

Chase was a large man, but when he sat up, the small bed the sorority expected me to sleep in looked tiny. Wouldn't be a problem with my bed back home, which I wasn't allowed to bring, because the bedrooms only had so much room.

"I don't have all night," he said while giving me a scolding stare.

"Like I said." Despite the way my pussy clenched, I returned his look with a sneer of my own. "Feel free to leave anytime."

I got up to go to the bathroom. Whatever the hell Chase did to me was halfway down my thighs. The only satisfaction I got was knowing that my orgasm got him too. His shirt was a little wet.

I, however, didn't have to wait to clean up. Problem was, when I stood up, my knees buckled. Thankfully, Chase didn't notice anything. He was too busy grabbing my hair and pulling me back down.

"Listen here, you stuck up, little cunt." His face appeared above mine, growling down at me. "One way or another, you're coming with me."

I glared right back at him. "No, you listen to me. I don't give a shit who you think you are. You're nothing to me. Less than nothing. Go order one of your little biker sluts around."

When his jaw clenched, I smiled a little.

"I wouldn't knock those biker sluts, Princess. They have something you don't."

"And what's that?"

Couldn't wait to hear this.

"Tact."

My eyes narrowed. I may not be the most pleasant person, but I could guarantee that I had more tact than those tube top-wearing hoes.

"Now here's what going to happen," his dark eyes met mine. "You're going to get your ass up, put some fucking clothes on, and walk out that door with me."

Keep dreaming, asshole.

"I could end you with a single phone call."

"Go ahead, Princess. Call daddy." Something about the way he snickered when he released his hold on my hair flipped a pit of unease in my gut. "Save me the trouble of letting him know I took my payment."

I sat up and eyed him. "What do you mean payment?"

"Daddy fucked up. Until he decides to man-up," he shrugged, "you get to pay the price."

He had to be bluffing. Daddy wouldn't get tied up in anything scum like Chase had their hands in. Our town was run by powerful men. All of which had my dad's back. They even made sure he stayed mayor.

"When Micha hears about this…"

"Who do you think sent me?"

My brows furrowed. Micha wouldn't do that, would he?

"I don't believe you."

"I don't really give a shit what you believe." Chase huffed out a sigh and pulled me across the bed. "And I'm done arguing with you."

Before I could blink, he had me hoisted over his shoulder and was walking out my bedroom door. This was a new predicament for me.

One I wasn't quite sure what to do about? Six-foot tall girls didn't generally get tossed over someone's shoulder. Staring at the floor, which seemed so far down, wasn't helping.

It took a few minutes for me to regain my bearings, but when I did, I went full force—kicking my legs while screaming and pounding into his back with my fists.

Know what that got me? Three hard smacks on my ass which was on full display, by the way, because someone tore off my underwear.

"Put me down, right now!" I demanded with a quick kick.

I could've gone completely feral, scratching and pulling his hair, but then I risked him losing his footing and both of us toppling to the ground.

And there was no need for me to get hurt. I mean, I didn't want to break a nail before I had my next appointment booked.

I turned my head and looked over my shoulder at the asshole carrying me, "This isn't funny."

"Do you hear me laughing?" Chase stated flatly.

Tanner stepped up behind us and smiled at me. "I say we gag her."

Managing to grab a statuette as we traveled through the entrance-way, I hurled it at Tanner.

"Gag this."

He easily ducked out of the way and tsked. "Didn't daddy teach you any manners?"

Oh, he wanted manners, did he? I'd give him all the manners he wanted as I ripped out his heart. Please tell me this hurts, and thank you for dying slowly.

Thankfully, I didn't have to dip into that uncivilized rage because, like a savior in an epic tale, Ava came running up.

"Wait," she yelled as the front door opened and cool air kissed my skin, "she'll need this."

Ava held up a bag, and my face dropped.

Saviour, more like evil sidekick.

"Ava?" I swung my hands over the man kidnapping me. "Do something."

"I did," she smiled and pressed the bag into Tanner's chest. "I packed you some clothes."

You've got to be kidding me!

When Chase stepped outside, I thought I'd have a few minutes before I was tossed in a creep van or something, but I didn't even get that because his damn bike was parked by the door.

No, I couldn't be taken away in a safe vehicle like a normal kidnappee. No, I had to get tossed over a damn Harley.

I tried once again yelling at my friend as Chase sat down on the bike, "I'm being kidnapped here!"

"Okay, bye. Have fun," Ava waved from the door.

"You are the worst friend ever!"

"Don't worry. I'll make sure someone takes notes for you."

Chase dropped me down in front of him, so my legs were wrapped around his waist, and I was staring right at him.

"I hate you," I hissed in his face.

"Hang on, Princess." With a loud roar, the bike came to life, vibrating up my bare ass. "It's a bumpy ride."

That's all the warning I got before he took off. The only thing I could do was bury my face in his chest and hang on for dear life.

It felt like I was trapped on that bike forever. The rush past, whipping over my skin in sharp cold spikes. The only warmth I got was from Chase's hard body, which I firmly wrapped myself around.

That didn't help calm down my pulse. My heart was fluttering wildly, expecting my body to be flung off at any second.

Every time he leaned to turn a corner, I squealed and clung onto him harder. When we finally came to a stop, I was so tightly plastered against him, I may as well have been a second skin.

Of course, that didn't last long. I lept off the bike and away from Chase faster than a kangaroo on steroids.

"What the hell is wrong with you?" I snarled while flinging my hands in the air. "You can't just throw someone on your bike and peal down the road like some maniac. Are you trying to kill me?"

Chase swept his hand over the Harley's seat, and held up his fingers. Displaying the glistening wetness I'd left behind. "You seemed to enjoy it."

I was tempted to yell that I'd almost pissed myself, except I would never do that. A lady was always proper and clean. Instead, I stamped my foot on the gravel ground and stormed away.

Yeah, it hurt walking on the rocky terrain, but that was nothing compared to ten hours in stilettos. So, bring on the jagged edges digging into my feet. I was going home.

Chase had other ideas. I'd barely made it two steps when I was scooped up in his massive arms.

"Where do you think you're going?"

I swung my arm up and slapped him in the face. "Away from you."

My strike barely phased him. So, I did it again, and again, and one more time, until he flipped me over his shoulder again. This time he at least had the decency to throw something over my ass.

Not that I cared if the men hooting and hollering behind me saw anything—I knew I looked good—it was the principal of the matter.

Chase walked us into the clubhouse, and up the stairs, past the room, I found him in yesterday. I wondered if the vase had left a mark on the wall. Hopefully, they'd cleaned it up by now.

The room we entered appeared to be a bedroom or some kind of apartment. There was a bed in the corner, some crappy ass old couch next to a wall, and what looked like a monitor or television.

I didn't get a chance to see well because Chase shrugged me off his shoulder and onto the most uncomfortable mattress. The springs squeaked as I bounced back against the headboard.

"Welcome to your new life, Princess," Chase waved his hand over the area, and I couldn't help but roll my eyes at the tack shell patterned wallpaper.

"Sorry to burst your bubble, but this is your life." I picked a piece of fuzz of the scratchy wool blanket and flicked it. "Mine doesn't have shag carpet."

His brows furrowed down at the floor. "What's wrong with my carpet."

So much, I didn't know where to start.

"I'll let you figure that out," I pushed off the bed and sprang for the door. "I'm going..."

I huffed out a sigh. On the other side, standing guard, was that big guy Chase had with him. His large hand reached out, shoved me back into the room, and closed the door.

"You're not going anywhere unless I let you."

I spun around and glared at Chase, who was leaning on a small desk with his arms crossed.

"Until daddy decides to play nice, your ass is mine. Every breath you take, every meal you eat, is because I let you." He rose and slowly stalked closer. "If I want you to get on your knees, you better damn well drop."

I cocked my hip and arched a brow at him. The day I got on my knees for this man was the day I burned my entire Jimmy Choo collection.

"The only words I want to hear out of your mouth," his gaze darkened as he stepped up and puffed his chest out, "are yes, Sir, and thank you, Sir."

Did he think this shit was going to scare me? Oh no, the big bad man was being mean. Please bitch, I reinvented the word mean.

"You're going to use me to get back at my father. Is that your brilliant plan?" I tore off my teddy and moved in the last few inches, pressing myself up against him. "Go ahead, Sir," I lifted my chin, rolling my eyes up to his, "use me."

The only response I got was a nostril flare.

"Huh?" I turned my back to him and sauntered away. "That's what I thought."

Two seconds later, I was face down on the mattress, with Chase's heavy hand pressing into my shoulder blades.

"You don't decide when shit happens, Princess."

"Whatever," I grumbled back at him.

My body sunk into the bed, preparing to take what was coming. Imagine my surprise when the only thing he did was clip a handcuff around my wrist.

"Night, night, Princess." He clicked in my ear before strutting across the room and out the door. "Get some sleep. You're going to need it."

I looked up at the metal chain attaching me to the iron headboard. "Son of a bitch."

Chapter 11

CHASE

It was a normal night at the clubhouse. My brothers were all here, playing games and having a few drinks. General all-around fun that I should be taking part in. So, why was I sitting here staring at a half-drunk beer when there was a hot as fuck chick chained to my bed?

'Because you're a good man. You don't want to hurt that girl.'

That was the problem. I did want to hurt Naomi. Got hard as hell just thinking about it.

'Don't do this, Chase.'

"Go away, Sam," I muttered and drained the rest of my glass. The bitter liquid burning down my throat did nothing to wash away my guilt.

I didn't feel bad for Naomi–bitch deserved what was coming. I didn't want Sam in the back of my head when I did it. She was gone, I knew that, but that ghost was all I had left. If she saw what I'd become...

My fingers snapped at one of the prospects for a refill as I turned my attention to Beast. A group of members sat around him, listening intently to the story he was telling. His hands swung through the air, explaining some great feat.

Funny thing was, when you took time to think about it, the feat wasn't that great. Beast just had a knack for stringing words together. I'd heard every one of his stories ten times over and would still sit down and listen. I'd miss hearing that big fucker talk when I left this world.

A glass full of beer was dropped down on the table. I nodded at Reggie, the prospect who brought it and took a long swallow.

Naomi was just a small part of my plan. Her daddy was the key to breaking down the Reapers business enough that my brother would be willing to cut a deal. Give The Lost Souls back their territory and leave them alone. In return, my brother would get me.

'You can't leave them again. They need you.'

I glanced at the patches around the room. Some were tarnished with age, while others were crisp and clean. I'd only patched in three of those. Beast and Mannix built this club back up. They survived my death once. I'm sure they could do it again.

'They will, but what about...'

My gaze shifted to Tanner, who was a few tables away, watching Beast talk. The first time I saw his eyes, they were hidden under black and purple bruises. The kid was so dirty, I thought he had black hair. It took a week of constant washing before the blonde started to show.

My old man thought I was crazy bringing him here, but what could I say? I liked the idiot. Any twelve-year-old that tried to rob a man my size had balls.

I don't know how he wound up in that alley or what happened to him. Whatever it was, it was bad enough that he latched onto a bunch of bikers. Little fucker even followed me to Ashen Springs.

'And now you're going to leave him.'

Tanner smiled as two of the sweet butts whispered in his ear.

"He'll be fine."

'The man I loved wouldn't do this.'

"The man you loved died eight years ago." I scrubbed a hand down my face and let out a sigh. "I don't know who the fuck I am now."

"You're Chase Mathers," Beast's wife, Jaz, dropped down in the chair next to me, "the kid I used to beat up on the playground."

I arched a brow at her. "Old ladies aren't supposed to be in the clubhouse."

"Careful, Spider," she reached out and grabbed my glass, "I still have that hockey stick."

That was a rough week. Not only did I get shit for having my ass kicked by a girl, but I couldn't see out of my eye for four days. I learned my lesson, though. Never pick on an armed redhead. Jaz made daily visits to make sure I was okay and warned me not to pull her hair again.

We'd been thick as thieves ever since. Beast used to give her so much shit. Until her curves filled out, then he gave her something else. The other guys respected her so much that they gave her a road name. Claire was her given name.

"Besides," She took a long swig of my beer and smirked. "I have to keep an eye on my man. Wouldn't want these skanks getting any ideas."

"Exactly why old ladies aren't allowed in the clubhouse."

"Just so you know," Jaz leaned in and whispered, "my blender's big enough for two sets of balls."

I snatched my glass back and chuckled. She probably had that blender sitting on a shelf so Beast would see it every day. Sam wasn't part of the club, and Jaz kicked my ass when she caught me with another girl...

I SIGHED *and pushed past Claire. "What are you doing here?"*

"Apparently, I'm saving your ass," She growled and followed me into the kitchen.

Jax, cocked a brow at us from the living room where he was playing a video game.

I threw open the fridge and cracked open a beer.

Claire slapped her hands on the counter. "Are you just going to ignore what I saw in there?"

"You didn't see anything." She interrupted us before it could get that far.

My dick was barely out when Claire came busting in my room. The chick I was with didn't even have time to lick the tip.

Claire flopped down and ran her pink painted nails through her red hair. "Why would you hurt Sam like this?"

My brows furrowed as I swallowed down my guilt. The entire time I was in the room with that chick, I could feel it burning through my veins, but I was doing this to keep Sam from getting hurt.

"That girl loves you."

Fuck, that hurt. Way to twist the knife deeper.

I sighed and dropped my elbows on the counter. "Do you know what I did last night?"

"It better not have been that bitch," Claire snarled over her shoulder towards the front door where my date had fled after the girl was slapped around, of course.

"I killed a man. Dragged him out to the swamp, slit his throat, and watched him bleed out. Sam doesn't love me." I pressed the bottle to my lips and let out a breath. "She doesn't even know who I am."

"So, tell her."

I snorted. Yeah right. Tell the sweet down-home girl with morals that I sold drugs, ran guns, and sometimes killed people for a living. I'm sure that would go over well. Her brother was a cop who'd arrested my ass three times since I started fucking his sister.

"You're an idiot; you know that." Claire shook her head, "That girl already knows what you do. She calls me every day to make sure you haven't been shot."

What? Claire was bluffing. Sam didn't know... Did she?

"If you want to lose the best thing that's ever happened to you, that's your choice," Claire pushed off the counter and walked away, "but I can't watch you do it."

I stared at the door after she left, wondering if I could have it all. Could I keep my girl and my brothers without risking one? I didn't want o give up Sam. Every time I closed my eyes, I saw her smile. No one looked at me like she did. I was the bad guy in other people's lives, but to her, I was the hero.

"Don't do it," Jax called out from his spot on the couch. "That girl is too pure for our world." He twisted his neck and looked back at me. "You're just gonna get her killed."

JAZ GAVE me one of her pointed stares. "Beast says you took that girl."

I rolled my eyes over at Beast and gritted my teeth. The fucker talked too much.

"What are you going to do to her?"

Whatever I want.

"Depends on her daddy."

"Chase," her small hand rested on my forearm, "Sam wouldn't want you to do this."

My gaze studied the concern sparkling in her bright eyes and then dropped to her tiny fingers clutching my arm.

"Sam's dead," I said, looking her right in the eyes, "because I took what I wanted."

Sorrow poured into her expression as her brows knit. "Chase..."

"Don't," I growled and pushed the chair back.

The legs screeched across the floor as I rose and walked to the stairs. I could feel Jaz's stare boring into the back of my skull as I left. It didn't matter what she thought. It didn't matter what anyone thought. I'd do what I had to do.

I creaked open the door, cautiously peeking in. One thing I'd learned about little Miss Queen Bee was not to underestimate her. I half-expected her to be standing behind the door with a lamp at the ready, but she wasn't anywhere near the door.

I almost thought she'd escaped until I stepped into the room and saw her curled up on the bed.

My head tilted, eyes zeroing in on her chest, watching the steady rise and fall of her breaths. Testing her, I took a heavy step closer. Not even a twitch.

If she wasn't asleep, she was a damn good actress. Then again, almost everything in her life was fake, including her smile.

I sat down on the edge of the bed and swept the hair off her face. What would that sultry mouth look like twisted in a real happiness? Had she ever known real happiness?

My hand slid over her shoulder and down her arm, pulling the blanket off her chest. She was so fucking beautiful, it hurt to look at her. Too bad she was such a cunt.

My eyes landed on her pert pink nipples. I lifted my hand and grazed my fingertips along the underside of her full breast.

Couldn't be a cunt when she was asleep.

'Don't take her this way.'

"Why not?" I whispered while gently coaxing Naomi to roll on her back.

She was my prisoner. I could do what I wanted with her, and there was a lot I wanted to do. Suck on her perfect tits while I finger fucked that hot little cunt again. I wouldn't fuck her yet. Not until the doctor called and gave me the go-ahead.

Most nights, I was drunk out of my mind, and God knows what I did. I may be an asshole, but I wasn't that much of an asshole.

Once I got that call, though, all bets were off. I rolled my eyes over the curve of her hip. I'd never been a big fan of anal, but fuck me, I'd like to give that ass a ride.

'Chase.'

I let out a long breath and tried to push the voice away. Sam couldn't be here. I needed her to leave.

She didn't.

'You're not this man.'

I tipped my head at the deep-set furrow in Naomi's brow. Her lips were pressed together in a tight sneer as if she was fighting something in her sleep.

'You should be protecting her. Not hurting her.'

That caused me to snort. "Yeah, sure."

Naomi Prescott was the last girl that needed protection. People should be protected from her.

'Look at her, Chase.' Sam's sweet voice called out, *'She's just as broken as you.'*

Chapter 12

NAOMI

My eyes fluttered open as a groan left my lips. Chase was passed out beside me, head thrown back with his mouth open. I knew I heard snoring. Bastard. I mean, he was an alright-looking bastard, but still a bastard.

A big bastard.

I tipped my head, watching his steady breaths. Each inhale expanded his broad chest, making him seem that much bigger. If he really wanted to hurt me, there wouldn't be much I could do to stop him.

A thought that, for some reason, caused my pussy to pulse.

Maybe it was the rough and gruff thing. I swear it was ingrained in female DNA to be attracted to brutes. The bad boy effect, I called it.

We could be in a room with charming, upscale men, and the instant some tattooed, muscle-bound asshole walked in, our pussies responded. And Chase was definitely a tattooed, muscle-bound asshole.

The black lines inked in his skin flowed effortlessly down his arms and around his hands. I wasn't big on tattoos, but his were kind of pretty. I could even make out a couple of names scrawled in the mouth of a skull dripping with lily petals. Sam and Maddox.

I hadn't heard those before. Were they part his big bad biker gang? Not very threatening nicknames if you asked me.

Oh, well. I didn't plan on being around long enough to find out.

I rolled over and scoured the room for a weapon. Anything I could stab him with would be fine. I'd even settle for a pencil. Worked in the third grade when Logan tripped me on the playground. I think he still had a scar from that?

Unfortunately, other than a lamp on the table beside me – which was just out of reach – there wasn't anything. I could always pry Chase's boots off his feet and beat him to death with those, but God knows what those things would smell like.

When guys like him wore boots, the outcome generally wasn't a pleasant aroma. One thing was for sure, the second I got the chance, I was throwing that tiny TV at him.

Guess it's plan B.

I sat up and stretched my free arm out as far as it would go. Then swung my palm through the air, bringing it down on his face with a loud crack.

Chase shot up so fast he rolled off the other side of the bed, hit the wall, and thudded on the floor.

Good morning asshole.

"Motherfucker." His growly face popped up, glaring at me over the mattress. "What the fuck…"

I smiled and sweetly sang, "I need to use the washroom."

"So go," he barked out.

My brow arched as I tugged on the chain attaching me to the headboard.

"Oh," he scrubbed a hand down his face and crawled back on the bed, "forgot about that."

Forgot about that? Seriously? How could he forget about someone chained to his bed? Especially if that someone was me. I mean, come on, look at me. I was hot. He knew it. I knew it.

Hell, the guys in his club knew it. Any one of them would give their right arm to fuck me, and he forgot!? I don't think I'd ever been this insulted. I was ready to slap him.

Until he pulled the key out of his pocket, then I wanted to slap myself.

"Who keeps the damn key in their pocket when they're sleeping beside their prisoner?"

Idiot. Did he want me to escape?

Chase clicked open the cuff around my wrist and cocked a brow at me.

"Are you lecturing me on how to kidnap you?"

"Well, someone should," I snarled and got off the bed. "Don't even know what you're doing. What kind of kidnapper are you."

I deserved better than some half-assed attempt at abduction. Tie me up, threaten me, make ransom demands, or at least have a place ready for Christ's sake.

Instead, I wound up in some after-school special. Next thing I knew, Chase would be teaching me some grand life lesson.

"You're the one that didn't check my pockets," he said, while laying back down and folding his hands behind his head. "Maybe you were too busy eye-fucking me in my sleep."

My teeth clenched as I glared back at him. I would never! Not with him. If anyone was eye-fucking here, it was him. I felt the heat in his dark eyes as he rolled them down my naked body.

"Looks like you're the one enjoying the show." I rested my hand on my cocked hip. "Like what you see?"

Because you are never getting it.

Chase yawned and shut his eyes. "I've seen better."

My jaw dropped. He did not just... I mean what did... he was... I can't believe...

"Ugh!" I snatched the blanket off the bed to wrap around my body.

Chase Mathers had no idea what he was talking about. What kind of girls did he hang around with? Skanks that's who. I marched off to the bathroom, muttering under my breath. Telling me he's seen better. Pfft.

He better be staring at my ass right now.

I snatched the bag Ava packed and slammed the bathroom door. Chase's words instantly left my thoughts. Was this a bathroom or an outhouse? The tub and shower were together and don't even get me started on the bright teal tiles on the floor. Teal?

It was awful. Did Riley grow up with brown counters and small sinks? It would explain her bad attitude. I'd be upset too. Who could live like this?

After making sure I'd covered the toilet in paper, I relieved myself and then carefully used my fingertip to turn on the sink. It groaned and creaked before spurting water out at me.

What fresh hell had I landed in? This was almost as bad as camping. At least I had some supplies.

I dropped the bag on the counter and unzipped it. Inside there were shoes, make-up, and clothes. All of which were Ava's. Not a problem for the make-up, the clothes, and shoes, however...

I dropped my face in my palm and sighed. Ava was barely five foot, and I was six. How in the hell did she expect me to fit in any of this?

The best I could come up with was a green Babydoll dress–that squished my boobs and was more of a shirt on me–and a pair of shorts I'm pretty sure she only bought because of all those 'look at my ass' videos floating around.

Gotta say, my ass looked pretty damn good, but when didn't it? Besides my escape plan wouldn't work if I was tripping over a blanket.

In the middle of the room, next to the sink, was a large window that just happened to be open. It was time to put all those years of cheerleading to the test.

Using the counter to steady myself, I slung one leg out the window sill and then the other. About a foot below was a roof that led to a small dip and another roof.

From there, I could use the gutter and swing myself over to a window, grab onto a lattice next to it, and climb down to freedom.

The only hard part about the first drop was doing it quietly. I flipped around and carefully slid down, softly touching my bare feet to the shingled surface. I might be able to squeeze into some of Ava's clothes, but there was no way her shoes were going on my feet unless I cut some toes off. I crept over to the dip and flattened against the wall when I heard voices.

The first one wafted from a window I had to pass by. "You got any twos?"

"Nah, man," another one said, "go fish."

My brows knit together. Go fish?

I ducked down and peeked in the edge of the window. Inside the small room sat two men in leather, playing cards.

"You got any tens?" the one with the big beard asked.

"How do you always get this shit?" The other one scowled at him and flung a card on the table. "You better not be fucking cheating."

Was I really sitting here, watching two bikers play Go Fish?

Beard boy chuckled. "Just lucky, I guess."

A groan drew my attention to something huddled up in the corner. All I could see from where I was, were a pair of bruised feet and legs. One of which twitched.

"Looks like he's awake."

Beard boy grunted and dropped his cards. "Let's see if he's ready to talk."

As tempted as I was to stay and see what was going to happen—I mean, they were playing Go Fish, how scary could they be—now was my chance to slip by the window unnoticed.

I scurried forward and quietly dropped down to the next roof. I was almost there but had to stop when three men circled the building. Flattening my stomach on the roof, I carefully shimmied back so they wouldn't see me if one happened to look up.

"You see that hard body Spider brought?"

There was that name again. Who the hell was Spider?

"How could you fucking miss that ass?" another one growled.

"Careful," a third one said, "Spider knocked Butcher the fuck out last night when he asked if he could have a piece of that."

Butcher, Spider, and hard body, I shook my head. Only men would get this worked up over a bike. It kind of made sense, I guess. We had shoes, and they had engines. Though I much preferred the shoes. You couldn't wear an engine to dinner, and they were dirty.

Once I was sure they were gone, I popped up and scanned the area. No one was in sight, so I headed for the window, grabbed the edge, and swung over to the lattice. From there, it was an easy climb down.

I was so impressed with myself that I even did a dismount. Kicked off the lattice, flipped in the air, and landed on my feet with my arms held high.

And that, folks, is how it's done.

"Uh-huh?"

The smile fell off my face.

Well, shit.

I turned around and came face to face with Chase. He was standing behind me with his arms crossed.

"You didn't think it'd be that easy, did you?"

"Whatever," I lifted my chin and pranced back inside, "at least none of my friends play children's games."

Chapter 13

NAOMI

Hell wasn't a blackened abyss of fire. It was a rundown hovel with shag carpet and wool blankets. True torment was being trapped in this room for hours on end. Unless there was a show people were talking about, I wasn't normally a TV person.

I didn't even know you could still get channels with an antenna. And let me just say, all that fighting to get the wires in the right direction, so not worth it. I couldn't even get a fuzzy picture.

I thought about climbing out the window again until I looked outside, and some of Chase's men smiled at me, which left me with one option. go through Chase's crap. He was a biker and, therefore, should have something interesting. Nope. The only intriguing thing I found was a few letters Riley had written him.

They were the typical, I miss you, we're doing okay crap all relatives wrote. Though, I wasn't sure if Riley was actually related to Chase.

For all I knew, he was just some creepy guy that liked to hang around her. Maybe he was doing her mom? Maria Adams was alright for a docksider, and she was drunk half the time, so it wouldn't be that big of a stretch.

I tossed the letters back in the dresser and moved over to the desk. Nothing there either, until I opened the bottom left drawer. There was a stack of papers inside. Docking slips and stuff like that from Ashen Springs.

It wasn't completely out of the ordinary for him to have this information. Chase did live in my hometown for years. There was no excuse for him to have my father's banking information, though.

What really got me were the discrepancies I found. I knew my father's accounts like the back of my hand. Hell, I had his credit card numbers memorized when I was twelve. But I'd never seen these deposits before.

Also, the payments to his lawyer each month were way too high. About ten thousand dollars a month by my calculations. Was daddy in trouble?

These records went back ten years, about four past when the deposits started. And each month, he overpaid his lawyer the same amount. Why? I flipped through the rest of the pages, looking for clues.

Everything seemed to point towards the money going in his account, not the overpayments he was making. I'm sure there was a reasonable explanation. People paid lawyers for all kinds of things, but that much a month, for at least ten years, seemed a little excessive.

"It's rude to go through other people's stuff."

I looked up to see a short girl with red hair and tacky jeans enter the room. A tray with a sandwich and a soda was held firmly in her arm.

"It's also rude to kidnap people." I sighed and went back to the papers I had spread across the floor.

"That, I agree with you on."

I arched my brow and eyed her. If she put in a little effort, she wouldn't be too bad—some eyeshadow, a little mascara, maybe some lip gloss. I'd never understood the tomboy thing. We were born with assets men lusted after. Why not use them?

"I'm Claire," she said, "but people around here call me Jaz."

"Why?"

"It's a road name."

Why did she seem proud of this? "Uh-huh."

She stood there for a second, staring at me, before holding the tray out and walking up.

"Brought you some food."

My lip curled at the sandwich. "I don't do carbs."

I did, had a bagel and cream cheese every morning for breakfast, but she didn't need to know that. Besides, I could only imagine what kind of toxic crap was in that sandwich.

I almost gagged when I had to watch Riley shovel spoonfuls of peanut butter in her mouth. Low-quality food for a low-quality person, I suppose.

"Oh," Claire set the tray down on the desk, "I'll remember to make you something vegetarian."

I fingered through my father's bank statements and said, "I eat meat."

"But not bread?"

With a sigh, I glanced up and nodded at the food she brought in. "Not that bread."

"Uh-huh." This time it was her brow that rose. "Look, I get that you're probably scared."

I snorted. It'd take a lot more than a pair of handcuffs to scare me. That kind of shit was Tuesday afternoon with Logan Hudson.

"But there's no need to give me attitude." She huffed and crossed her arms. "I'm trying to be nice here. You could at least be kind back."

I sat back and eyed her cocked hip. She wanted me to be kind did she?

"Claire is it?"

She nodded.

"Can I give you a piece of advice?"

Moron smiled back at me. "Of course."

"Just because you dress like a guy doesn't mean I'll let you fuck me."

The smile fell off her face just as fast as it came.

"I see. You're one of those."

This should be interesting.

Her mouth twisted in a scowl. "I've met girls like you."

"I highly doubt that." There were no girls like me.

"All you sliver spooned barbies have one thing in common."

I sighed, "And what's that?"

"You wouldn't know a good thing if it slapped you in the face."

A good thing? How in the hell was this a good thing? I hope she wasn't implying…

"Are you talking about Chase?" The very thought of the man curled my mouth in a sneer.

"Chase is a good man," she insisted.

Right, he was so good, he kidnapped me. Not to mention all the other stuff. Spanking me and kissing me. Good men did not humiliate people.

"You don't know anything about him."

I didn't want to know anything about him.

"You know what, I hope he does hurt you." She stomped her foot and spun around. "You need a lesson in manners."

She slammed the door, and I rolled my eyes. What did I care what some biker whore thought? Chase Mathers and his whole gang of thugs could fall off the face of the earth, and it wouldn't make a difference to me. I didn't care what he did.

I looked up at the laptop on his desk. Well, a little information couldn't hurt. What was that saying? Know thy enemy?

Picking myself up off the floor, I gracefully sat on the edge of the chair behind his desk and flipped the laptop open.

Hmm, I need a password.

I tried the regular things. Riley's names, his birthday, which I found on some papers in his dresser, and the name of his tattoo parlor in Ashen Springs.

I was just about to give up when I remembered the names on his arm. Maddox granted me access.

Of course, it wasn't connected to the internet–why would my luck start now–but one file did catch my eye. It was titled auditions.

I clicked on it.

Three different video files popped up. T and J, Sweet butt party, and breaking in Grace. I clicked on the last one because I recognized the tattooed arm hanging in front of the camera.

The picture came to life, and a girl walked into view. Chase's voice could be heard behind the screen.

"Get on your knees."

The girl obeyed and demurely dropped down.

"That's it," Chase came into view, walking up to the girl and running his fingers through her dark hair. "Always so obedient. Are you my good girl, Grace?"

The girl, Grace, I assumed, lifted her chin and peeked up at him through fluttering lashes. "Yes, Daddy."

Chase tsked and pressed his finger to her lips. "Is that what you call me?"

"I'm sorry," she bowed her head in reverence. "I mean yes, Master."

I couldn't stop staring. I'd played games like this before, but this was different. The way Chase gazed down at her with a combination of authority and adoration. How her entire body sagged when he tsked? She really didn't like disappointing him? Why? What did she get out of it?

He clapped his hands, making me jump along with Grace.

"Eyes up here!"

I shifted in the chair. Something about the tone of his voice got to me. It stirred something.

"Bratty little slut, I should spank you."

My fingers tightened around the edge of the desk.

"You'd like that, wouldn't you?"

Grace licked her lips and nodded. I couldn't help but remember the first time I met Chase. What his hand felt like coming down on my ass, over and over again.

'What do you think you're doing?'

'Teaching you the lesson your daddy should've.'

"All fours now," Chase barked out, "I want your ass in the air."

Grace didn't waste a second. She dropped her face down on the ground and stuck her ass up in the air. I waited in eager anticipation as Chase walked off-screen and then came back with his shirt off.

My eyes traveled over the dips and groves in his torso and down to the V dipping into his jeans. He really was built well.

He sauntered over to Grace, roughly yanked her pants down over her hips, and then smoothed his palm across her ass.

Just spank her already. What was he waiting for?

"Is this what you want?"

Grace whimpered and nodded her head.

"You want me to turn this ass red?"

"Goddammit," I slammed my hands down on the desk in frustration. "Just do it already."

"Just do what?"

I stopped dead and slowly lifted my gaze. Tanner was standing in the doorway with his hip cocked against the frame. I quickly slammed the laptop shut.

The corner of Tanner's mouth curled. "What were you watching?"

"Nothing."

"Oh no, no, no, Princess," he pushed off the door and waltzed his way across the room. "You seem to forget I fucked mommy."

My eyes narrowed.

"So?" Who hadn't? My mother was well known to the slum kings in my hometown. "What does that have to do with anything?"

He flattened his palms on the desk and leaned in. "You both have the same flush in your neck when you're ashamed."

How dare he! I was not ashamed, and I sure as hell wasn't anything like my mother.

"What do you want?" I snarled back at him.

"I came to get you, Sweetheart. Chase has had enough of daddy's bullshit."

Good, I'm glad daddy was giving him a hard time. Still. . .

I eyed him and crossed my arms. "What do you mean you came to get me?"

A slow smile spread across his face.

Chapter 14

CHASE

A small bell rang out as I opened the door to the dinner. Mannix and I weren't typically the kind of guys you'd see in a fifties-style diner, but this one happened to be owned by his sister.

So, most people only gave a small glance. The few that were gawking at us like a bunch of lookie-loos were either tourists or new customers.

"Little brother," Fiona's face lit up, "I wasn't expecting to see you today."

Mannix let out a breath and grumbled, "I hate it when she calls me that."

I gave him a nod. Being a little brother myself, I understood where he was coming from. I don't think any younger siblings liked having their little status pointed out. It was as if our older brother or sister was saying, I was here first.

Fiona swept her hands on her apron and waved at two empty stools, "Have a seat."

The age difference between Mannix and his sister was an obvious one. The lines in his face came from the grumpy expression he wore, whereas hers were from age. Fiona was fifteen when Mannix came along.

That didn't mean his parents were any less capable. Unlike most of the guys in the club, Mannix had an ideal childhood. Loving parents, little league, and a date to prom.

Why he decided to join up with us, I never understood. Then again, I guess we all had our secrets. Though I suspected this had to do with Janey. The girl he met one summer and never talked to again.

"What can I get you guys?"

I gave his sister a smile, "One of your fabulous burgers and a vanilla shake would be great, Fee."

"Sure thing. " She returned my smile and skipped off to the kitchen, not waiting to hear what her brother wanted, which deepened Mannix's already sour mood.

Couldn't blame the guy. Normally, newer members were sent out on the drug trafficking jobs, but we'd had a few problems with this particular dealer. Meaning, founding members should be the ones to pay him a visit this time. Mannix and I were volunteered for the job. Fucking Beast.

I had no doubt that this was all his wife's doing. Jaz had been trying to sneak a peek at Naomi, and I wouldn't let her.

"Stay the fuck away from her," were my exact words.

Jaz liked to talk, and I didn't need that princess knowing anything about me other than where to bend over–I liked spanking her–when to shut up, and when to sit the fuck down.

I was deep into my burger when Mannix's mood shifted. His entire face went hard as he dropped his fork and slid off the stool. All it took for me to understand was one glance over my shoulder. Three men sporting skull and cross bone patches waltzed in.

My eyes zeroed in on one in particular. The scar across his cheek caused my fists to ball up. Harris. The motherfucker that shot me eight years ago. Once upon a time, he was my old man's confidant.

Now he was my brother's. Scum is what he was. He didn't just abandon his brothers. He stabbed them in the back. It was Harris that killed the Lost Soul members who refused to patch over. I knew this because Beast's little brother was one of them.

I rose from the stool and instinctively went for my gun. Mannix shot me a look and shook his head, which made me stop. This was his sister's place, and unlike the Reapers, we respected family.

Harris's eyes lit up when they landed on me. "Well, who do we have here?"

"Don't fuck with me, Harris." The only reason this prick would be here was if he knew I was. "How long have you had your boys watching the place?"

"Can you blame me? It's not every day I get to see someone rise from the dead."

"Guess you're losing your touch."

"You too. I thought for sure you'd find that bomb. Told your brother to strap it to your hog." He tipped his head and smirked. "Then again, I guess you can't take a baby on a bike."

This motherfucker!

Rage poured me like lava. Lighting up my senses to the point that I didn't give a fuck about the innocent bystanders watching from their tables, that is until I heard another voice. One I hadn't heard in eight years.

"Should've never had a baby in the first place."

Jax.

"I told you, you'd get her killed." My brother's dark gaze locked with mine from across the dinner. "Should've listened."

I couldn't see anything but him and that serious line in his brow. The last time I saw him, he wore that look…

8 YEARS AGO:

"*If it isn't the prodigal son.*"

I shoved Beast, "Fuck off."

Fucker knew I hated that shit. It was the older members' way of poking fun at my old man. My teenage years weren't as kind to me as my brother. Jax was always a tough motherfucker. Built like a brick house with a smile that could charm any girl out of her panties. When kids at school talked about the badass Mathers brothers, they weren't referring to me. The biggest fight I had through puberty was with acne.

Beast slapped his hand on my shoulder, "How's your bitch doing?"

"Don't call her that," I growled, slapping his big mitt off me before shooting him a smirk. "She's doing great."

At seven months pregnant, Sam was constantly smiling. I must've lucked out in the wife department because mine didn't have any of the bitchy symptoms I'd heard guys complain about. My Sam was as big as a whale and even more perfect than the day I met her.

"Look at the smile on this motherfucker," Harris sauntered up and pinched my cheeks. "Little Chasey-Wasey is gonna have his own pipsqueak."

I ripped my face out of his grip and snorted. "Prick."

Why my old man kept him around was beyond me. If old ladies were allowed in the clubhouse, he would be the reason I didn't bring Sam. The sweet butts came to my old man on more than one occasion, complaining about Harris's happy hands. Hence his road name. Happy Harris.

"Hey, Chase."

I frowned at the look on Kickstand's face. He was one of the older members who got his name from the fact that no one wanted to park beside him. His hog was always the first to fall. He was also my old man's best friend.

"How's he doing?"

Everyone standing around me in the clubhouse dropped their gaze. That wasn't a good sign.

"Not good." Kickstand nodded at the door leading to my old man's office. "Jax is already here."

I'd never been more scared to walk into a room in my life. My old man had been diagnosed with lung cancer three years ago. The doctors gave him six months to live, and we thought he beat it.

Three months ago, we were proven wrong. His health degraded quick. He lost weight, could barely walk, and needed an oxygen tank to breathe.

The shell of a person who was left wasn't anything close to the man who raised me. I hated seeing him like that, but Sam was right. He needed to be surrounded by his loved ones. Jax took it harder than I did.

My brother wasn't around much. I couldn't blame him, though. They'd always been close. Closer than I had been with him. It had to be hard on my brother.

My heart dropped when I stepped into the room and saw all the medical equipment. Even with his failing health, my old man refused to abandon the club. So we turned his office into a room for him. Even found a nurse that didn't mind coming out here to take care of him.

"Hey, dad..." I stopped when Jax looked up at me and shook his head.

A tear rolled down my brother's cheek and fell to the floor, splattering into a fat wet spot. For half a second, I panicked, thinking I was too late, but my old man rolled his gaunt face my way and smiled.

"Chase," he called out in a weak tone, "come here, my son."

I held the tears back as I walked over and slowly took the chair next to my brother. "Hey, dad."

I wanted to tell him he looked good, that everything would be okay, and he'd beat this. But the defeat in his eyes told me he already accepted his fate.

"My boys," His gaze shifted between my brother and I, "my time in this world is almost up."

"Don't say that," Jax growled. "You'll beat this."

Our old man smiled and lifted his arm to tap my brother's cheek. "You can't go on hating the world, Cory. You need to let me go and find something that makes you happy, son."

My brother dropped down and hugged my old man, clinging to him like he used to do when we were kids. It broke my heart to see him like this. I wanted to protect him from this pain like he protected me on in the school-yard. But I couldn't.

Death was something no one could fight, just survive the aftermath. So, I did what I could and placed my hand on my brother's back so he'd know he wasn't alone.

"I'll take care of the club, Dad," Jax cried into his chest, "I promise."

"No." Our father gazed down at my brother's head. "Your brother will do that. I need you to guide him."

"What!?" We both called out in unison.

THAT WAS the last time I saw my brother. He got up and stormed out. By the time our father had left this world, he was gone along with Harris and a few other members.

"Leave, Jax." Mannix must've sensed my need to lunge at him because he flattened his palm on my chest. "Now."

Jax smiled and walked across the room, taking his time to eye up every person watching us.

"Why would I do that?" He paused at a table occupied by three college-aged girls, and snatched a fry off one of their plates. "Family reunions are all the rage."

I glared at his mouth as he chewed the stolen food and prayed with all my might that he would choke.

Once he swallowed, he gave the girls a shrug. "Guess my brother doesn't agree."

"You leave my customers alone, Cory Mathers." Fiona appeared from the back, waving a rolling pin.

"Hey, Fee," Harris perked up, "Still got some spunk, I see."

Mannix grumbled under his breath. His sister didn't need protection, though.

"You take that smile out of my dinner, Harris," Fiona pointed the rolling pin at him, "or I'll shove this rolling pin up your ass."

Jax narrowed his gaze on Fee. "You should watch your sister Mannix. I'd hate to see her wind up in a bad situation."

"You should leave," my growled warning wasn't an empty threat. I would shoot him in the head right here while everyone watched.

"And *you* should've stayed dead." His eyes met mine as the room went quiet. "You have something I want, little brother. Let her go."

So, Jax knew I had the princess. It was my turn to smile. "Let who go?"

If I didn't know better, I'd say Jax was worried. Why?

"Careful, Chase. Bad things happen to pretty little things all the time." Jax spun around and headed for the door. "Just ask the girls at Pi kappa."

I crossed my arms and leaned against the counter as my brother and his men left. Harris paused halfway out the door to give us a smile and wink.

Prick.

"Son of a bitch," Mannix muttered, "Did Jax just threaten a sorority house?"

"I think so."

Was I surprised? A little. After everything I'd seen my brother's men do, I still hoped the man I thought he was, was still in there.

That didn't mean I'd underestimate him. Empty threats weren't Jax thing. Which meant the girls at Pi Kappa were in real danger.

"What are we gonna do?" Mannix asked.

"We have church in a couple days. In the meantime, we'll have someone keep watch over the place."

Mannix cocked a brow at me. "What about that bitch?"

I assumed he meant Naomi. The term bitch was made for that girl. "Don't worry about her."

"Uh-huh?" His tongue clicked off the roof of his mouth. "How long's it been since you've seen your brother?"

I got where he was coming from. Jax hadn't so much as said boo since I reappeared nine months ago. Kind of convenient that he came out the day after I took her.

Whatever he was worried about had nothing to do with her daddy, otherwise, Clive Prescott would already be dead. The only question was, what did Naomi know, and did she know she knew it?

Mannix crossed his arms and looked right at me. "We need to know what's going on in that town."

"I couldn't agree more." I slapped my hand on his back and smiled. "Don't worry, I'm on it."

"Are you?"

Fuck yeah, I was. The doctor called to give me the go-ahead this morning. So, I was about to be all up in that shit. Torturing the information out of a woman, even one like Naomi, wasn't something I wanted to do. Ever.

I would if I had to—it wasn't just her life on the line anymore. There were other girls in that sorority house, but there were also other ways to break her, ways that would get me off instead of turn my stomach.

It was time to teach that little bitch, who her master was.

Chapter 15

NAOMI

I tore my arm out of Tanner's grip and snarled, "Don't touch me."

"You're the one that wanted to put up a fight." He shrugged.

Was he really surprised? Of course, I was going to put up a fight. These assholes kidnapped me. Well, one asshole did, but the rest were complicit, and that was just as bad. If not worse.

I stopped in the hall and crossed my arms, to which Tanner raised a brow.

"You sure you want to play this game again?"

As much as I would love putting him in his place with a kick to the nads, I'd already tried that. I also tried slapping him, biting him, and scratching him. Guess how many strikes I landed?

Tanner wasn't as big as Chase–I don't think anyone was–but he still had bulging muscles. It wasn't fair that he was also deceptively graceful. He dodged every single one of my attacks and pinned me on the ground in under two minutes.

"Well, Princess," the corner of his mouth lifted in amusement. "You wanna go for round two?"

My gaze narrowed on the smugness sparkling in his bright eyes. If I didn't hate him before, I sure as hell did now.

"Ugh, whatever." I waved my hand and walked down the hall, taking the lead despite not knowing where we were going. I'd be damned if I was going to let Tanner lead me anywhere.

Squirrely bastard.

Tanner tsked and tipped his head to the right when I turned to go left. My eyes rolled in displeasure, but I followed his directions.

My bare feet padded on the cold floor, sending a shiver up my legs with every step. God, I missed my heels. Hell, I'd be satisfied with clothes that fit. I was still wearing the makeshift outfit I'd put together. Freaking Ava.

I hope she was enjoying this because when I saw her, I was going to kick her ass.

"This way, Sweetheart." Tanner threw his thumb down a dimly lit hallway.

I eyed the door at the end. Where the hell was he taking me? A damn dungeon? We were in the basement of Chase's club quarters, or house, or whatever the hell he called it.

It was shitty upstairs, and it was shitty down here. Though I did have to admit, the cement walls and floor I was walking through did give the basement an eerie ambiance. I almost missed the shag carpet.

Tanner stopped next to the door and leaned against the wall. "Go on."

"What's in there?" I asked while staring at the brass doorknob. The door was black, which didn't exactly bode well for what was on the other side.

I grew up around shady people and learned early on that the color someone chose for something could tell a lot. Micha, for instance, his entire room was black with splashes of red, and that man had some dark desires.

Nothing like Logan Hudson there was seriously something wrong with that boy. Not particularly surprising given who his father was.

Chase was different. The last thing I expected him to have was an ominous corridor of death with a black door at the end. I didn't like it when people were unpredictable.

That's when you wound up with the happy school teacher, singing *'Sunshine, Lollipops and Rainbows,'* as she mowed down a mall full of people.

I cocked my hip and nodded at the door. "After you."

"Aww," Tanner popped his bottom lip out and sang, "is the princess scared?"

"I am not scared." Just a little unsure. "I don't get scared."

"Uh-huh."

I scoffed at the disbelief openly displayed on his face, though it was the spark of amusement that pissed me off. With a firm eye roll, I swung open the door and stepped inside.

Huh?

I stood there stunned for a second as the door clicked shut behind me. This room was kind of elegant, filled with black leather furniture and plush purple pillows.

My eyes swung from a pair of manacles hanging on the wall in the corner to a large four-poster bed at the far left end.

I'd seen a room similar to this once when Micha took me to his father's 'club.' There were various playrooms set up in the underground of Malum.

This, I was not expecting, and I was slightly concerned. Why did men always set these places up in basements? Was there something wrong with the sun?

"What took you so long, Princess?"

I was so busy gawking at my surroundings that I hadn't noticed Chase on the right side of the room. My brow lifted as he pulled a tripod out of a bag. Was he...

"Are you setting up a camera?"

He completely ignored me and continued pulling out equipment.

"I am not letting you film me."

Chase lifted his head and cocked a brow at me. "Let?"

Yes, let. Who the hell did he think he was? I wasn't one of his little shanks.

"If I did do video—which I don't—you would be the last person I did it with."

It wasn't a complete lie. I had done a video or two with Micha and Logan, but those were personal. If they got out, they had just as much to lose as I did. What did Chase have?

Worn-out jeans and a shag carpet. Shag! I still couldn't believe that. Come on, biker boy, join the rest of us in this century.

"Let's get one thing straight." He straightened up, rolled his shoulders back, and strutted over to me. "You'll do whatever the fuck I tell you to. Wherever I tell you, whenever I tell you."

Is that so?

I stepped right up and glared in his eyes. "Or what?"

"Or daddy will get a better video than I had planned."

That's what this was about. Chase would try and make me cry, so daddy would break and give him what he wanted. Fuck that. I wasn't going to help him do shit. If he wanted me to fight him, then I'd do the exact opposite.

Activate sex kitten mode.

I dropped my head enough so I could peek up through my fluttering lashes. "You gonna teach daddy a lesson?"

He gave me nothing in response. No twitch in his stern expression, or glint in his stare. Just a huff as he crossed his arms and leaned back, saying, "That's the plan."

Hum. That usually worked. Guess I'd have to dive deeper in my seductress repertoire. Spotting a whip hanging on the wall behind Chase, I sauntered slowly around his large frame. Making sure to put an extra sway in my hips.

"Are you going to hurt me?" I purred and reached out to stroke the whip. Delicately caressing the leather strands as I glanced over my shoulder at him, "Rough me up a little?"

The first cracks in his stony exterior started to show. I had to hold back a smirk as Chase forced a swallow down his throat and licked his lips.

"What are you doing?"

"You wanted me to put on a show." I made my way to the bed and wrapped my fingers around one of the posts. "That's what I'm doing."

Chase's gaze darkened as he rolled his eyes down my body and back up. Something about the way he was staring at me, with that same glint in his deep brown orbs that I saw in the video, caused a shiver to wrack through my system. For half a second, I forgot what I was doing until he cleared his throat.

"What kind of show are you going to give me, Princess?"

Was he calling my bluff? Alright, let's see you call this Mr. Mathers.

"What kind of show do you want?" I pulled my bottom lip in my mouth and crawled up on the bed. Surprisingly this mattress was soft. Why the hell didn't he sleep down here?

"Should I finger myself again? Get my pussy nice and wet? Or maybe," I arched my back, presenting my ass, and gave one cheek a firm swat. "You want to spank me?"

God, please spank me.

My brows furrowed at my thought. That video I came across may be stuck in the back of my brain, but that didn't mean I wanted the brute to spank me. My gaze landed on Chase's large hands, twitching at his side.

Right?

How was he so calm? If my heart was pounding a mile a minute, then his should be visibly throbbing. He should be panting right now. I was practically serving myself up on a silver platter. How many girls of my caliber would even play this game with him.

Pay attention, Naomi. You're in charge here. Not him.

My lips curled as I slid off the bed and stalked back over to him.

"You seem confused, Mr. Mathers." I could've sworn I heard him groan. "Maybe you want me to do something to you?"

I stepped up to him and dragged my finger down his chest. Tracing lightly over the hard ridges under his shirt. A plain white Walmart t-shirt should not look that good on anyone.

"Don't get any ideas, Princess." Chase grabbed my ass and yanked me up against him. "You're not that good an actress."

Pushing my anger down–no one called me out–I slid my hands around his hips and grabbed a handful of his ass. "I'm not acting."

Which was a real problem because a large part of me wasn't playing a façade. I literally had to stop myself from moaning a little at the firmness of his ass.

"You wouldn't be trying to get me to finger your hot little cunt again, would you?"

Dirty talk should not be this hot.

"Oh, no," I gave him my best pout and lifted up to whisper in his ear, "this is about you."

"Uh-huh." Chase leaned in, grazing the rough hair on his cheek against mine. "Prove it."

I reared back and glared up at the smug smirk on his lips. Did he think that would scare me off? That the possibility of having to touch him would make me run away and hide under the bed like a child.

He obviously didn't know me at all. *I* didn't back down. Ever. If I had to, I'd take this shit all the way. It was just sex.

Or...

Keeping my eyes on his, I slowly lowered to my knees. Once I was down there staring up at him, Chase arched a brow. I could practically hear the challenge in his thoughts.

My hands moved to his belt, unfastening the buckle while pulling the leather strap through the loops. If he thought he was going to win this, he was wrong.

My stomach flipped as I opened his jeans, and his dick sprang free. It was a lot bigger than I thought. I might've gasped a little when the angry head jumped out at me. Who doesn't wear underwear?

Someone who's planning on fucking the shit out of you, that's who.

"Well, Princess, are you just going to stare at my dick," Chase tipped his head, causing a lock of brown hair to flop to the side, "or are you going to do something with it?"

Was I going to do something with it? I'll show him what I was going to do with it.

My hand shot out, wrapping around his hard shaft, and oh my god, was it hard. And hot, and thick, and smooth. Everything a nice cock should be and then some.

I couldn't stop myself from stroking him. Tightening my fingers as I pulled my hand along his length and twisted just a little at the head.

This time Chase openly groaned, which not only spurred me on but caused my pussy to clench.

He got harder in my hands as I continued to work him while watching the tip of his cock glisten with precum. I'm not sure why or what demon possessed me, but for some reason, I leaned in and licked him, scooping up the drops with my tongue.

"Fuuuck," Chase groaned and speared his fingers in my hair.

No guy had ever reacted this way when I touched him. I mean, they liked it and got off, but Chase was almost feral like he didn't just want me to touch him he needed me to. I was mesmerized by it. And a tiny bit afraid.

"This is a one-time thing," I said, not sure who I was trying to convince, "it's not going to happen again."

Case rolled his eyes down at me and panted out, "Whatever you say."

"I mean it," I reiterated.

"Sure thing."

He wasn't getting it. Just because I might be slightly attracted to him didn't mean I was going to give in. This I'd chalk up to an experiment.

"Don't go expecting me–"

"Naomi," Chase said, cutting me off.

"What?"

"Shut up and suck my dick."

My jaw dropped. He did not just say that. Yeah, okay, it was kind of hot, but you didn't talk to a girl like that, especially one that had your dick in her hand.

"You listen to me," I snarled up at him, "no one talks to me like…"

"Oh, for fuck sakes," Chase growled and shoved his cock in my mouth.

I tried to pull back, but his grip on my hair was so tight, all I could do was hold onto his thighs and ride it out.

"Jesus fucking Christ," he ground out, making me gag on his length, "can't you shut your fucking trap for once?"

I muttered back a response that even I couldn't understand. My mind was too occupied with how he felt thrusting down the back of my throat. I was high class.

This shit shouldn't be turning me on, but it was. The harder he fucked my mouth, the wetter I got.

"You're so fucking infuriating." *Thrust.*

"I want to beat the bitch out of you." *Thrust.*

"String your ass up and whip you until you fucking listen."

I moaned despite myself, which spurred Chase on. His face twisted in a combination of hatred and pleasure as he pounded into my mouth harder.

I don't know when things shifted, but at some point, I joined in my own abuse. I wanted to please him. Not because I needed to win, but because when I met his gaze, I saw something. A spark that ignited a feeling deep inside. A sense I didn't know was there. Possession.

He roared out his orgasm, spurting his release down my throat, and all I could think was *mine*.

Chapter 16

CHASE

I sipped on my beer and glanced at the stairs for the hundredth time. My apartment was up there. It wasn't the place I was avoiding, so much as the girl locked inside. I'm sure she didn't want to see me either, not after what I did.

I hated Micha Kessler for being that guy. The one that didn't give a shit about consequences. It didn't matter to him what Riley wanted or what she thought. He just took her, which was exactly why I didn't get involved. Because it did matter to me, if Riley wanted my help, she would've asked for it.

Can't get involved if you're too busy hiding.

That wasn't it. I'd do anything for my niece. For fuck sakes, I came back from the dead for her. I didn't question it or think about what would happen once my brother found out I was still breathing.

I just did it because Riley needed me. Like what happened with Naomi. I did it because I had to break the bitch somehow.

She started the whole thing. Prancing around, playing her little game of seduction. When she climbed up on the bed back arched with her ass in the air… I could've taken her right then, but I didn't. I held back.

Then she smacked her fucking ass. God damn, I couldn't get that image out of my head. Green eyes glittering at me as her hand swung through the air and came down on that firm fucking cheek.

That was the only reason I mouth-raped her. Besides, she wouldn't keep her fucking trap shut. Had to shut her up somehow. It had nothing to do with how good it felt shoving my cock down her throat. It was a matter of principle.

Who the fuck was I kidding? I was no better than Micha Kessler.

I dropped my head in my hand and scrubbed it down my face. Riley was going to kill me if she ever found out about this shit. I should let Naomi go, but I couldn't. And what was more, I didn't want to.

I liked knowing she was up there, sitting on my horrid floor, waiting for me to come back. After all, men like me didn't ask for what they wanted. They just took it.

I looked up at Beast as he walked into the lounge, with a big smile on his face and a lipstick mark on his cheek. That fucker and his wife were so in love it was sickening. They'd been that way since puberty smacked us all in the face. Just watching them together made my teeth hurt.

'You can be that happy too, Chase.'

"Go away, Sam," I hissed and pounded back my beer.

Snake flattened his palms on the table and cocked his head. "We got a problem."

I sighed. Of course, we did. "What is it?"

"Tex says there's a group of girls headed to the clubhouse."

I glared up at Snake. "What the fuck do you mean they're headed for the clubhouse?"

"Apparently, one of them stuck a shiv in Cannon's leg when he refused to let him pass."

"Some chick stabbed..." I stopped and shook my head. "Let me guess, tiny as fuck blonde?"

Snake reared back in shock. "Yeah? How'd you know."

About this time, I heard high heels clicking up the stairs—a lot of high heels.

"Let's just say this isn't the craziest thing she's done."

Pushing the chair back, I stood up and headed across the room. I got to the stairs just in time to see Ava leading a group of girls up the last flight. My arm shot out, cutting her off.

"What are you doing?"

She looked up at me with a big smile. "It's hazing night."

"Uh-huh?" I cocked a brow at the girls behind her, half of whom were looking around and wringing their hands. "And you decided to haze them by seeing how many times they could get raped?"

"Of course not," she scoffed and waved her hand through the air, "that would just be mean."

Right?

I took a deep breath and tried again. "Ava, this is a biker clubhouse."

"Yeah?"

I closed my eyes and pinched the bridge of my nose. What the hell was wrong with this chick? "I don't think this is a very safe place to bring these girls."

"Oh, no," she placed her hand on her cocked hip and waved her finger in my face, "Naomi is not getting out of this."

Leaning over, I looked past her at the four large men in leather staring hungrily up at the group. Unless she had a twin, I'm pretty sure Ava was there when I took Naomi.

She even packed her a damn bag. If she brought these girls here and disturbed my men's sanity because she forgot about the night, I kidnapped her friend...

"Naomi can't go with you."

She didn't say anything, just stared blankly up at me.

"You get that, right?"

"Uh-huh," she nodded.

I paused and eyed her sparkling eyes. Was she up to something? I knew her brothers. Parker was pretty tame, but Preston didn't do shit without a reason.

Aside from Louis Kessler, Preston was the one person I kept an eye on in Ashen Springs. His coldness was almost as lethal as his intelligence. I wouldn't put it past his sister to be just as methodical.

"If you think bringing these girls here is going to make me let Naomi go…"

"Oh, no, she's not getting out of that either."

Okay. Wasn't quite sure how to respond to that?

"Okay, let me get this straight," I crossed my arms and leaned my shoulder against the wall, "you brought these girls here because it's hazing night, which Naomi is part of, and you don't want me to let her go?"

"That's right," she said as if this was the most normal thing.

Huh?

"Alright," I shrugged and moved aside to let them pass. This shit, I had to see.

The girls clicked past, swinging their large eyes round with fright and curiosity. A few of them looked like they wanted to make a run for it, and they might've if there wasn't a group of muscle-bound men following them up the stairs.

One of whom was Tanner. Though I wouldn't call what he was doing following. Fucker was running up the steps like his life depended on it.

"Hey," he propped his arm up on my shoulder and hunched over out of breath. "I heard my future wife is here?"

Hoots and hollers roared through the air, echoing down the stairwell.

"In there," I nodded at the lounge.

"Thanks," he slapped my shoulder and limped towards the open door.

"Do me a favor and kick the sweet butts out." There was about to be a roomful of drunk horny men, and those girls did not need to see that shit.

Tanner's brows knit as I began to climb the stairs. "Where are you going?"

"To get Naomi," I muttered, "apparently, it's hazing night."

Chapter 17

NAOMI

Chase said my presence was requested, and I expected to be taken back to the dungeon, which I wouldn't have minded. It had a better decorator than Chase's crappy apartment.

That's not where he took me. Nor did he answer my questions about why he left me alone in said crappy apartment all night and all day. I suppose I shouldn't be surprised. Disappearing after they got what they wanted was just something men did.

When he waved me into the bar/lounge type room, my brow rose. The girls from my sorority were huddled in the corner whispering. I spun around with my hand on my hip. If Chase thought I was going to let him hurt them in any way, he had another thing coming.

"Why are they here?"

He nodded at Ava, "Ask your friend."

I curled my lip at him as he strutted past to join Tanner and the big guy at a nearby table. Tanner winked at me, and I flipped him off, which only caused a big smile to spread across his face. I turned my attention to Ava, ready to ask her what the hell was going on, but she beat me to it.

"Okay, girls," she snapped her hands at my sorority sister, "let's do this."

Was this some kind of rescue plan? Ava must be in her right mind because this was kind of genius. I'd never seen men this quiet, and there were a lot of men packed in this room.

I didn't know Chase had this many guys in his club. Every possible seat was occupied, leaving some to stand in the back. It was eerie, actually, standing up by the bar with a bunch of big burly men staring at us.

Hmm, maybe this wasn't a very good rescue plan after all? Hard to slip out unseen when everyone was watching us.

"Ava," I paused when I noticed the girls lining up in front of the bar. This was either the worst rescue plan ever or... "What's going on?"

"It's Wednesday." She scoffed while giving me a 'duh' glance.

"Okay?" Why was Wednesday a big deal? Did Mr. Chang have a deal on spring rolls or something? Even I had to admit they were really good spring rolls, better than any of the food I'd gotten here.

Ava let out an exaggerated sigh. "Hazing night?"

My face dropped. Hazing night? Seriously. I was being held captive in this craphole, which my friend obviously knew about, and she was worried about hazing?

"Ava," grabbing her shoulders, I turned her to face me, "you remember the other night when that asshole threw me over his shoulder?"

"Yeah. That's the same night I took Bill's gear. That guy does not know how to play cards, by the way. I only had a pair..."

Well, that explained the helmet and shoulder pads.

"Hey," I gave her a little shake, "I need you to pay attention."

Ava straightened up and nodded. "Got it."

"That night when I was taken, that was a kidnapping," I explained, not that anyone in their right mind wouldn't already know that.

"Okay."

"I need you to call someone, like your brother." Preston could get me out of here.

"You want me to call Parker?" Her nose scrunched up. "I mean, I could, but he's got the babies, who are so cute by the way. Did I tell you? I found the cutest little jacket for Weston..."

This wasn't getting me anywhere.

I snapped my fingers in front of her face. "You need to get me out of here."

"Oh." Her eyes widened with realization.

That's right.

"Yeah," Ava shook her head, "I can't do that."

What?!

I threw my hands up. "Why not?"

"You remember when we helped Logan with his date?"

I rolled my eyes. How could I forget? We didn't just help Logan arrange things–for a guy with an insane amount of charm, he was completely obtuse when it came to the female species– that was also the night Ava tricked me into a date with Chase. At least I had mace then.

"What does that have to do with anything?"

"Well, Logan is an idiot, but you're more stubborn," she declared and walked away.

What?

This better not be some fucked Ava logic thing. It wasn't cute this time.

"We're waiting," she sang back at me.

"You can't be serious?" The look on her face told me she was dead serious.

I'm not sure what was worse, the fact that not one of the other girls said a thing or the men impatiently staring at me? Like I was holding up some grand production. In their case, it was more likely a game of beer pong or go fish.

Who above the age of ten played that game, unless they were a parent, of course? Not my parents, that's what nannies were for.

"Get the fuck up there!" someone yelled.

My eyes narrowed on Tanner. Pretty sure it was him, and based on his smug grin when Ava thanked whoever did it, I'd say I was right. Congratulations, Asshole, you just made it to the top of my shit list.

Letting out a defeated breath, I sauntered up next to my Mayberry roommate, who still had her hair in pigtails. What the hell else was I going to do? Run? I could pull those pink scrunchies out of her head.

Did the girl not have any fashion sense? Get rid of the jeans and put a dress on for once. A cute little skirt would be better than what she was wearing.

Long sleeves in Miami, who did that?

"Are you okay?" Bailey whispered over at me.

"Do I look okay?" I shifted my unimpressed gaze her way. "I'm wearing a Hello Kitty T-shirt, for Christ's sake."

Chase brought me some clothes, all of which I'm sure were from some backwoods thrift store. They were better than the tiny clothes Ava packed me, though.

"I think it's cute."

I sighed and rolled my eyes. *Of course, she did.*

I was so ready for this day to be over with. Who knew? Maybe Ava would come to her senses and decide to help me after all.

It became evident that wasn't going to happen when she instructed all of us to strip down to our underwear, so she could circle our imperfections with a magic marker. Not a problem for me–I didn't have any imperfections–the other girls, however...

I was about to argue until I saw Chase grinding his teeth. He was not happy, and since I was down for anything that made him unhappy, I stripped my clothes off.

The underwear I was donning wasn't anything close to what I would've picked. Bows on panties? What was I twelve? That didn't mean I wouldn't rock that shit.

I locked glares with Chase, peeled off my shirt, and pushed the jeans over my hips. His nostrils flared as most of the other girls followed suit, and the men in the room came to life—whistling and hooting and hollering.

Mayberry and one other girl were the only ones that didn't join in with the rest of us. They stood there red-faced and clutching onto their shirts. To be fair, I was pretty sure Bailey was a virgin.

She wouldn't even change in front of me. I wasn't sure about the other one, whose name was Lane, I think. She was pretty quiet, I'd only seen her a couple of times around the house.

"Come on, girls," Ava's gaze shifted from one to the other, "I want those clothes off, or else." She pulled the Pi Kappa paddle out of her purse and smacked it on her open palm.

"Fuck yeah," someone in the crowd growled.

I rolled my eyes. *Neanderthals.*

Bailey still hesitated, but the other girl lifted her shirt over her head.

"What the fuck?!"

Everyone turned to stare at a guy that just walked in. My eyes narrowed, pretty sure he was the someone that flipped me off the other day.

Whoever he was, he was pissed as hell. His light eyes burned so intently with rage, I could feel the heat.

His arm raised, pointing firmly at the girl who'd just taken her shirt off. "Put your fucking clothes back on, Lane!"

"Cole?" Her eyes widened in horror as she quickly snatched her shirt up and held the cloth against her chest. "W-what are you doing here?"

"What am I doing here? What the fuck are you doing here?"

"Well… Ava… I mean…" she stammered while glancing around the room. Probably for help. I could step in, but why? This was entertaining. "My sorority…"

"Fuck your sorority!" Cole barked out, "If your ass isn't outside in two minutes, I swear to fucking God…"

That was all Lane needed to hear. She jumped out of line and scurried down the stairs faster than crowds on Black Friday, which was saying a lot. Those sale shoppers were crazy.

"Hey!" Ava called out, taking a few steps closer to the angry man.

This might be an interesting night after all. Like most of the others here, Cole was a big guy, but he'd never met my friend.

"Don't," Cole growled at Ava.

Oh, someone was protective.

"What are you," Ava popped out a hip, "her brother?"

"No, my best friend is," he spun around and stormed out the door. "Stay the fuck away from Lane."

I was defiantly getting to know that girl now. She might just become my new best friend since mine clearly didn't have my best interests in mind.

"Make the blonde one take off her bra!"

I assumed the prick that yelled was talking about me. Besides Ava, I was the only blonde up here. Cammie was kind of blonde but more red than blonde. Strawberry. I cocked my hip and glared out at the crowd, prepared to say something. Chase beat me to it.

He shot out of his chair, slammed his hands down on the table, and snarled, "Who the fuck said that?"

The entire room got quiet. Even I didn't know what to say. Men looked at me all the time, and no one had ever gotten mad about it.

"I said, who the fuck said that?"

In the middle of the room, a few men backed away from another, who I assumed to be the culprit, based on the way his eyes widened when Chase stormed over.

"I'm scared," Bailey clutched onto my arm. "We shouldn't be here."

"Ugh, calm down." I absently waved my hand at her. "We're fine."

At least I thought we were. Chase looked like he was going to kill that guy. Murder wasn't something any of these girls would be able to handle seeing. Luckily that big guy and Tanner stepped in.

Each one grabbed an arm and slammed him back against the wall. And even then, they had a hard time holding him at bay.

"Let me go," Chase growled.

"Sorry, brother," the big one growled back. "Can't do it."

It was kind of hot watching Chase's muscles bulge as he fought the other men.

The man Chase was glaring at stood up. "What's the big deal?"

"Get the fuck out," Tanner twisted his head and looked over his shoulder at the other man, "before *I* shoot you."

I was with that guy. So he said some typical guy crap. What was the big deal? Though he didn't seem very impressed about it, he did leave, grumbling under his breath the whole time.

Chase was only let go when he was out of sight. He ripped his arms out of the other men's grip and rolled his neck. Good, maybe now we could get this shit over with.

Apparently, that was not what he had planned.

Chase snapped his eyes my way as he marched across the room and grabbed my elbow. "Come on."

"Brute," I smacked his arm and fought back against his pull. "Let me go."

"Don't fuck with me, Princess."

Don't fuck with him?

"You brought me down here for hazing," I shot Ava a scowl, who was sitting back and watching with a smile, "so hazing is what I'm going to do. Now, if you don't mind…"

The next second I found myself staring at the floor as Chase tossed me over his shoulder.

"Fuck hazing."

He carried me up the stairs and dropped me on the desk in his apartment. A lamp crashed on the floor as my back landed on the hard wooden surface.

"Oh my God," I snarled at the pain radiating up my tailbone.

His hand shot when I tried to get up and wrapped around my neck.

"Shut the fuck up! Just keep your mouth fucking shut for once." I felt fire lick across my skin as his rage-filled glare rolled down my body. "Prancing around in a room full of men in this shit."

His grumble was so quiet, I wasn't entirely sure if he even knew he was talking. Either way, I'd had about enough of this shit. There was absolutely nothing for him to be angry about. These clothes were the ones he brought me.

"What the hell is wrong with you? Are you jealous or something?"

"Yes."

I stopped. What? I'd seen guys get jealous. Logan was king in that department. He'd go off if someone just looked at his girl, but I'd always chalked it up to his instability.

Normal guys didn't act that way. Sure they might be envious that someone got to fuck someone else. They get all feral and possessive. At least they never had over me. My eyes narrowed in suspicion as I searched the deep lines of Chase's scowl.

"Why?"

"What the fuck do you mean why?"

I don't know what his game was, but I wasn't going to fall for it. So I decided to call him on it.

"Why are you jealous?"

The scowl on his face twisted into a look of confusion. This time it was his gaze that searched mine. I lay there, watching his mouth open with silent words only to close again. When he finally did speak, it wasn't anything close to what I expected.

"Who hurt you?"

Chapter 18

CHASE

I asked her who hurt her and know what she did? She slapped me and said she was the one that did the hurting. Naomi was a bitch before, but after that, she was an utter cunt.

There was no talking to her, no calming her down. I couldn't even look at her without setting her off. So I left her alone and spent the night in the dungeon. That didn't mean I slept.

I lay there awake most of the night, running through what had happened.

Was I jealous? Yes, I fucking jealous. If I'd have gotten my hands on Axel, I'd have killed the motherfucker. Seeing Naomi standing up there with goddamn bows on her panties set me off. I don't know why?

It wasn't like I cared about the bitch, unless hate counted towards that. All those guys staring at her, and then Axel had to go and open his fucking mouth. I just lost it. Maybe I had too much to drink?

Now I couldn't stop thinking about what she said.

'Why?'

Who asks that? What happened to her to make her think she wasn't worthy of jealousy? And who the fuck did it? Micha? That little prick Logan? She used to hang around with them. Did one of those assholes hurt her?

"We're all here," Beast nodded at Tanner, who dropped down in the chair next to him, "let start this shit."

I scanned the seven faces sitting around the table. All of the older members were sporting a diamond one percent patch. Tanner somehow weaselled his way in, no one had ever questioned him being here either.

"We're waiting for one more."

Though they all cocked a brow at me, it was Mannix that spoke.

"Who?"

Their confusion was understood. Church was sacred. It was where we discussed the club's activities and future. Who did what, where shipments were sent, and other illegal actives. Every single man here paid for their place at this table in blood. They were trusted, valued, and loyal to a fault. Newbies were not invited. In this case, though...

"I invited Roach."

The argument started instantly.

'He can't be here.'

'He's too young.'

"He hasn't been patched in for a year.'

I let them mull it out and made my way to the bar to pour myself a drink while I waited for them to finish. It wasn't quite noon yet, but after the night I had, I could use a shot or two. The last time this room erupt like this was when my old man got sick.

I couldn't help but think how Jax and I should've seen his choice to put me in charge coming. No one except Harris wanted to follow my brother. He was reckless and cruel. I still believed in him, though, until he took everything from me.

Beast slammed his fist on the table, silencing everyone, and twisted his gaze my way. "What were you thinking? Roach is too new."

"He also has a personal investment in this week's topic," I pointed out.

Tanner was the only one who didn't mutter something. He sat back with his arms crossed because he already knew. I talked to him about this last night.

After learning that Roach's best friend's little sister was in Naomi's sorority, we decided he should have a say. The only person Roach talked about was his friend, which in our eyes made him family, and family was to be respected.

"Is this about last night?" Kickstand's eyes rolled up to mine. He wasn't the same Kickstand that acted as my old man's second. He was one of the first Harris took care of, but he got the name for the same reason. "She's just his friend's sister."

"The same friend he did time for." That shut them up.

Snake brought Roach in. They met in prison while Snake was doing time for a crime he didn't commit. We offered to take care of the little bitch that put him there.

He wanted to do it himself. So, I told him to let us know if he needed back up and left it up to him.

About this time, the door opened, letting sun cascade across the floor as Roach walked in. Some of the guys weren't happy that he was here, but no one said anything. That is until he sat down beside Mannix.

"Don't expect this to be a regular occurrence." Mannix grumbled in his usual grumpy tone.

Always respectful of the order around here, Roach simply responded with, "I'm honored to be involved."

Mannix grunted and propped his boot up on the table.

May as well get this shit started.

"As you know, Jax has threatened the Pi Kappa girls." I walked around the bar and rejoined them at the table. "The question today is what are we going to do about it?"

A few of the guys suggested we keep watch on their house, more suggested they move in here. After last night's hazing episode, the girls stuck around and hung out with the guys for a while.

It took a bit for the fear to wear off some of them, but once it did, they warmed right up. Being treated like a regular person left a lasting impression on some of the guys.

"I say we hit the Reapers," Kickstand said while raising his fist in the air. "Take out one of their supply houses and show them we mean business."

Roach's brow rose. "Won't that just put the girls in more danger?"

"Not if Jax is more worried about us."

Beast nodded at Kickstand's statement. "He's got a point."

He did. My brother was more of the 'What is this costing me now?' versus 'What can I get in the long run?' kind of guy. Planning ahead wasn't his forte. There was one thing they were forgetting.

"If we hit one of his stash houses it'll be all-out war."

More than one responded with, "It's already war."

"Not like this." I shook my head. "If we do this, you need to be ready to get shot walking to the store. Or check your hug before you roll it over. And as for family…" I forced down a swallow and looked them all in the eyes. "Jax doesn't give a fuck about family."

Not even his own.

"Are you prepared to put everyone you've ever loved in danger?"

The murmurs started again and quieted down when Tanner piped in.

"No offense, Boss. I know what he did to you," my hand fisted on the table, "but we have to do something."

"Agreed." Mannix sat up and braced his arms on the table. "The problem isn't Jax's lack of morals it's that he doesn't take us seriously. We need to make him."

"It's not our families he'll come after," Beast lifted his chin and rolled his eyes my way, "it's you."

They didn't know my brother like I did, but there was clearly no talking them out of it.

"Alright," I let out a breath and scrubbed a hand down my face, "let's do it."

It wasn't like I had anything left to lose except my life which I was more than fine with. We decided on one of the Reapers' less guarded stash houses and wrapped up the meeting. Just as the last man was leaving, my phone went off displaying a call I'd been waiting for.

I nodded at Tanner as he closed the door, and I answered the call.

"Clive, took you long enough. You must not care very much about your daughter."

Naomi's old man's voice rang out from the other end. "I could have you shot, Mathers."

I snorted out a chuckle. "Better men than you have tried."

"What do you want?"

Right down to business, then. Good. "What is my brother moving on the Aroura?"

"I don't know what you're talking about."

Shit was going to hit the fan after the raid tonight. I didn't have time for this shit.

"The longer you fuck me around, the more fun I'm going to have with your daughter."

Clive countered with, "How do I know you haven't done something to her already?"

"You don't."

"Then why should I do anything you say?"

That was a valid point.

"I could send her back to you in pieces." Also, a valid point. "How would your wife feel about getting her kids' fingers in the mail?"

"She could survive that."

Was he fucking serious? What kind of father lets their kid get tortured for someone else's cargo? What the hell was Jax moving in that boat?

Naomi's reaction last night came back to me, and I couldn't help but wonder if her father was the one that hurt her? It takes a sick man to let their kid get chopped up.

Then I remembered something else.

"What are you afraid of, Clive?"

My brother told me to let her go. Why? She wasn't the one making deals with him. What did it matter if I had her? Because it wasn't Clive breaking that had my brother scared, it was the fact that Naomi was with me.

"That I'll kill your daughter, or that I won't?"

"She's just a girl," he said and hung up.

That's when I heard a squeak behind me and turned around in time to see a flash of blonde hair.

Fuck.

Chapter 19

NAOMI

I don't know how long I ran for. There was no direction or place I was trying to reach. I just wanted to get away, away from Chase who was calling my name, the people who supported him, and my dad.

My feet pounded against the ground along with my heart, but no matter how fast I ran or which way I turned, I couldn't outrun that voice.

'She's just a girl.'

Daddy wouldn't pass me over like that. I knew he wouldn't. He just wasn't going to give into my abductor. Never give in to terrorists. That was his motto years ago when I told him about Ryker, and it was still his motto now.

The only time people had power over you was when you gave it to them. Crying over something that already happened wouldn't change anything. It just made you look weak.

I broke through the treeline at the back of the compound and hunched over to catch my breath. This place was a lot bigger than I thought. I couldn't hear the rumble of bikes anymore or any of the people calling, and I still hadn't reached the end of it.

Or maybe I had? It was possible the chain link fence didn't surround the entire place, and I did run through a group of houses.

I highly doubted a motorcycle club would have houses on their property. They were a bunch of rowdy guys that liked to drink and fuck. Not exactly Pleasantville material.

The setting sun cast a pink glow across the water in a small lake to my right. I watched two birds take flight, heading for a small cluster of trees on the other side.

They flew overhead, twisting and turning around each other as if it was a game. Perhaps it was?

I envied those birds playing in the sky, without a care in the world. Who did they have to impress? Their world didn't rely on a carefully perfected persona. No one cared what they wore or how they acted. They were free to be who they wanted and do what they liked. I didn't even know what I liked.

A glint to the left caught my eye. That's when I noticed a house. The green roof was barely visible through the treeline.

The forest wasn't as thick here, but in the fading light, the building blended into the plant life. If the sun hadn't sparked, I might never have seen it. I dusted my hands off on my jeans and walked towards it.

Maybe they had a phone I could use? Daddy would come and get me if I called. I mean, I did get myself into this situation. So, it was up to me to get myself out of it. Part of that, I could blame on Ava and her incessant need for spring rolls.

But like the day I chose to talk to Ryker in the park, none of this would be happening if I'd just ignored Chase.

I entered the backyard and paused when I stepped on something hard. One good thing about the cheap sneakers Chase bought me, I could run. They were thin as hell, though.

I could feel every dip and groove in the ground. In this case, the groove was a hammer. At first, I thought someone had forgotten to pack it up until I noticed that it wasn't lying in the grass. The grass had grown around it. And the hammer wasn't the only tool I saw.

Screwdrivers, chisels, and a toolbox lay around the rusty pieces of a swing-set. One of the swings and part of the slide had been put together and then just left. My brow furrowed at the house.

One of the chains on the swing was broken, leaving the wooden bench to rest lopsided on the deck. Other things stood out to me. Crooked shutters along with a dried-out hot tub. The gutter was well maintained, though, and there wasn't a speck of dirt on the deck.

It was weird. Like someone cared about the place but didn't. The perfect two-story house with an eerie ambiance in the middle of the woods. This was the kind of place people walked into in horror movies.

Luckily for me, I wasn't in a horror movie, and mutated, cannibalistic hillbillies didn't live in South Miami. A fact I almost reconsidered when I opened the back door.

There wasn't a crazed killer waiting on the other with an ax in hand or human body parts on the table. The interior was actually kind of homey. It had everything a house like would. Refrigerator, stove, and cute furniture.

Like the small kitchen table, complete with a highchair and vase in the center. That's not what threw me. It was the long-dead flowers in the vase and layer of dust coating everything.

The entire place was like that. Room after room of empty, forgotten memories frozen in time. Where had everyone gone, and why were there still clothes in the closet? I ran my hands over one of the dresses hanging in the master bedroom.

Whoever the woman was that lived here, she was about my size and had decent taste. The blue material wasn't something I would wear–it was probably last in style about nine or ten years ago–but it was cute.

My suspicions were confirmed when I found a bottle of *Emeraude* on the dressing table. That perfume had been discontinued for some time now. Bottles could still be bought online, however, most were knock-offs, which I could smell from a mile away.

What was in here was the real deal and probably worth a pretty penny. It wasn't something someone would just leave behind. Especially a woman. When we found our fragrance, that was it. We would kill someone to get our hands on the last bottle.

Who were these people?

My curiosity led me deeper into the dwelling. Searching through rooms and opening doors, I stopped when I came upon a nursery. In the corner of the room sat a toolkit toybox full to the brim with toys.

The other side housed a changing table fully stocked with diapers and creams. My heart just about broke when I looked in the crib and lifted the blue blanket. Nestled underneath was a stuffed Harley.

It was tucked in so perfectly I could see the baby's arm tightly wrapped around the body of the bike. I could even smell the baby powder in the air.

The rocking chair in the corner creaked against the floor, drawing my attention to blue block letters resting on the dresser. Maddox. The same name I saw on Chase's arm. I walked across the room and swept the dust off a picture on the wall.

My breath hitched when I was met with a pair of familiar dark eyes. A younger Chase stood in front of this house. Next to him was a woman with sandy hair and dark blue eyes, but it was the baby in his arms that I couldn't stop staring at.

"You shouldn't be in here."

Startled, I clutched my chest and sprang back. Tanner was standing in the doorway, with his shoulder resting on the frame. His eyes weren't sparkling like they usually did. They were dripping with sadness as he stared at the picture I'd cleaned off.

"Her name was Sam." He pushed off the doorframe and stepped up to the portrait. "She was a good woman, took me in and treated me like her own. No one had ever done that for me before. I was disposable to everyone, but not her. Or Chase."

I looked past him to the eyes of the woman. They seem almost familiar?

"I'd probably be dead if it wasn't for them."

I couldn't stop myself from asking, "What happened to them?"

"They died." Tanner let out a long breath and spun around. "Chase's brother killed them."

His brother? Why would he do that? They were his family too. Chase was his brother. How could he do that to his own brother?

Family was supposed to stick together. Lift you up when you fell down, and be there to help you through the hard times. They weren't supposed to be the hard times.

'She's just a girl.'

My gaze tipped to the crib and stuffed Harley lying inside. "How old was he?"

"Six months."

God.

I swept a tear off my cheek and sucked in a breath.

"You ever seen a man spiral? I mean really spiral. Completely destroyed with nothing left to lose? Cause I have." Tanner picked up the stuffed Harley and continued, "I watched this destroy Chase. I saw him paint the streets red with blood," his eyes rolled up to mine, "and then I saw him give up."

"Why are you telling me this?"

He sighed and crossed his arms. "Because I think you can fix him.

What?

"You're crazy." I scoffed, "I can't fix him."

The man lost his family. No one could fix that.

"Yes, you can," Tanner insisted. "I used to think it would be Riley that pulled him back, and for a time, she did. But the way he looks at you is the same way he used to look at her."

I rolled my eyes. "Now I know you're crazy."

Chase hated me, which was fine. I hated him too.

But do you?

"After everything you've seen, you still don't get it." Tanner snorted and shook his head.

"Get what?"

"Look at this place." His arms swung around, spanning the room. "Chase hasn't been able to look at this house, let alone step inside. It hurts too much. Micha risked his life for Riley, hell, even Logan. He handed himself over to the monster from his childhood to protect his girl."

Ava told me about all of that. How Ryker came back and took Riley and then Shelby. She was scared, and I couldn't blame her.

What he did to her was nothing compared to what the rest of us went through. What any of that had to do with this, I didn't get.

"Ryker's dead." I pointed out, "and I highly doubt he had anything to do with what happened to Chase."

Don't get me wrong, I wouldn't put it past that sick bastard to hurt a baby, but Chase didn't show up in Ashen Springs until like eight or nine years ago. *Around the same time, that dress was new.*

"How can someone so smart be so stupid?"

"Hey!" I'd been called a lot of things bitch, cunt, uptight, but stupid wasn't one I'd stand for. "I was in the top ten percent of my class, on the honor roll, and was asked to attend three ivy league colleges."

I was not stupid.

"Alright," Tanner sighed and scrubbed a hand down his face. "Let me ask you a question."

This should be good.

"What's the most important thing in life?"

Pfft. That was easy. "Reputation."

"No, Princess." He shook his head. "There's only one thing that makes this shit life worth living."

I huffed and crossed my arms. "And what's that?"

"Love."

Really? That's what he was going to come back with?

"Love doesn't exist."

At least not in the way he was talking about. The very idea of soul-mates was ridiculous. Marriage was an agreement, a business deal between two people. Humans were social creatures.

No one wanted to be alone, so they found someone they could tolerate, and even that only lasted so long. That's why infidelity and divorce rates were so high. Everyone was so desperate to believe in love.

Problem was, people weren't destined to be together. They simply put up with each other.

It was a man-eat-man world. The only person one could truly rely on was themselves. My father taught me that because he didn't want me to grow up with some romanticized idea of how things should be.

"If you can look around this house, see all these pictures and memories covered in dust, and still tell me love doesn't exist," he shook his head and walked out of the room, "then you're more broken than him."

Chapter 20

CHASE

I kicked out the stand on my hog and looked up at the rundown Ferris wheel. Most people wouldn't notice the light glinting off something in the top red bucket. Then again, most people wouldn't expect someone to be sitting up there with a sniper rifle. I

n any other city, a rundown amusement park would be a mecca for illegal teenage activity. There was a reason the kids around here avoided this place, and it had nothing to do with the haunting rumors.

Was this place haunted? Yes, but not by a ghost.

This was the last place I wanted to be. Well, second last place. I spent hours looking for Naomi. Don't think I'd ever been so glad not to find someone in my life. She heard what her father said.

What the hell was I going to say to her? Sorry? Your dad's a tool? Didn't quite seem like enough. Besides, the raid was in two hours I had more important things to do.

I stepped off my bike, triggering a spotlight to click on and blind me.

"Shit," throwing my hand up to shield my eyes. I called out, "Come on out, you paranoid fucker."

Three more spotlights turned on, flooding the area in brightness so intense, God himself would be impressed. A few seconds later, a mound of rubble to my left shifted and lifted off the ground.

I cocked a brow as Wilder stood up, turning what I thought was a pile into some kind of blanket draped around his shoulders. A blanket that looked like a pile of rubble.

Black streaks were painted around his face, framing a gaze that I could only describe as yellow or golden. They weren't dark enough to be brown or bright enough to be green.

Everything about the man was like it couldn't make up its mind. His hair for example, which he had piled on the top of his head in a bun. The locks were brown and red. It was the deadness in his face that got me every time. People called Preston void and empty, but none of them had met Wilder.

He dropped the butt of the rifle in his hand on the ground and braced himself against it. "You here to dispose of something?"

"No." I shook my head.

"Too bad." He kicked the gun up, slinging it over his shoulder, and strutted across the cement path to the haunted house. "The gators are hungry."

I watched him disappear inside and thought about leaving. The chances of convincing him to help me out were pretty slim. The only thing I had going on my side was the fact that he owed me a favor.

I caught the crazy motherfucker wrestling a gator last month. He had the thing pinned with his arm locked around its jaw. Why? Who the fuck knows? He could've been hungry. He could've been bored. One thing he wasn't doing was paying attention.

Wilder didn't see the asshole with a gun sneaking up on him. But I did.

With a sigh, I followed him into the haunted house, which looked nothing like it should. The inside had been transformed into an actual livable space. Couch, TV, and woodburning stove. He even had a little table with two chairs in the corner. One of which I sat in.

"What's with the flowers?" I asked, nodding at an empty soda can with three dandelions in it.

Wilder shrugged off the blanket and said, "People like flowers."

"Do you like flowers?" I was legitimately curious.

He looked me dead in the eyes. "No."

My brow arched. Alright then. Wilder wasn't just an odd duck, he was the odd duck. Most of his life was spent in the military. Black ops or some shit, I think. Other than claiming the government had a hit out on him, he didn't talk much about it.

I didn't believe that shit until I saw the dog tags on the prick that was trying to kill him. He didn't so much as twitch an eye at that.

Even now, he didn't react. I could tell he was uncomfortable with me being here–Wilder didn't like it when people invaded his space. He just poured some water in a kettle and put it on the stove.

"You're probably wondering why I'm here?"

Again, I was met with silence as he reached up and pulled a tin off a shelf.

I had to be careful how I worded this. You owe me a favor, so do it wasn't going to fly with him. There were very few people in this world I was afraid of. Wilder didn't have the girth to his form that I did, but the man was all muscle.

Every time he moved, I could see the bulges gliding under his skin. He could tear me apart with his bare hands and not even break a sweat. That wasn't the issue. Death I could handle. Hell, I welcomed that shit.

The problem came with how long he'd make me suffer first.

"I'd like to call in that favor?"

He turned around and stared at me while gracefully dipping a teabag into a mug of water.

I waited a second for him to speak before I continued. "There's a war coming."

Wilder sipped his tea.

"My brother is taking things too far."

"You want me to kill him?"

It was unnerving how normally he asked that question.

"No," I shook my head. That was my responsibility. "There's a sorority house he threatened." Here goes nothing. "I need you to keep an eye on the girls there."

I held my breath and stared at the head of a snake tattoo winding around his shoulders and down his left arm. It felt like the viper's eyes were watching me as silence grew heavy in the air.

The only sound trickling through the room was the small sips he took from the mug in his hand. Even more disturbing was the fluffy little orange kitten wrapped around the ceramic, with the words hang in there written across the top. How's that for irony?

I was just about to get up and leave when he finally spoke.

"How many girls?"

Did that mean he was going to take the job? "A dozen. Maybe more."

"How long do you want me to watch them?"

"I don't know?" My brows furrowed as I gave him a shrug. "Guess that depends on how long the war lasts."

Wilder walked over to a sink in the far corner and washed out his mug.

"I'll give you a week," he said while carefully placing it back on the shelf.

"Great." Hey, a week was more than I hoped for, gave us some time to breathe. "I appreciate this."

He gave me a nod as I turned to leave.

"Oh, and Chase."

I stopped in the doorway and glanced back at him.

"The next time you come in my territory unannounced," His dead eyes met mine, "I'll shoot you in the leg."

"GET DOWN!" Beast yelled and pulled me behind a car as bullets cut into the metal.

An explosion went off from inside the building behind us. The raid went off without a hitch. We rode in, took care of the Reapers inside, and made off with their stash. The problem came when backup arrived.

Two of our men were hit. Beast, Mannix, and I stayed behind to get them out before the whole building went up in flames.

Both those men were dead now, burning inside a two-story house in the middle of suburbia, and Mannix had taken two in the leg.

"Great time to put Playboy on babysitting duty," Beast growled over the roaring flames.

"Stop whining and fucking shoot," I snarled while leaning around the hood of the car and popping a few off.

Fact was, Beast was right. Tanner was a pain, but I swear that kid had a horseshoe shoved up his ass. I'd seen him get out of shit that no fucker should've survived. I left him to find Naomi because I didn't trust anyone else.

That girl was fucking up my judgment. I was so concerned that someone else might touch her, that I benched our star player.

Mannix groaned and reached out to grip my leg. "Get me on my fucking bike."

"In case you haven't noticed," Beast's big mitt slapped down on Mannix's fresh wound, "you're shot idiot."

"Barley," He tsked. "Pussies can't aim worth shit."

"Yeah, genius," Beast lit the wick on a Molotov cocktail and tossed it over the car. "Stand up."

The glass bottle shattered on the pavement in a flash of fire, igniting one of the Reapers' legs.

"He's right," I called over to Beast, "we have to get the fuck out of here."

I could hear sirens in the distance, and we wouldn't be doing anyone any good locked up.

Beast growled out a loud, "Fuck," and stared through the cloud of black smoke to our bikes. They were parked maybe a hundred yards away.

Making the trek to escape wasn't ideal, but we'd run out of options. Something that Beast seemed to understand as he wrapped Mannix's arm around his shoulder and lugged the fucker into the black smoke.

I stared back at the burning building where my men's bodies were. One of them had a kid and the other a wife. What was I going to tell them? Those men were my responsibility, and I didn't even have a body for their families to bury.

'Those men made their choices.' Sam's sweet tone rang through the back of my head. *'You did what you could.'*

"Did I?"

I could've pushed them out of the way or at least brought their bodies back.

"Spider," Beast waved back at me, "let's go."

Taking one last at the fire, I pushed off the car and followed Beast. Bullets whizzed by, hitting the ground, but somehow we made it to our rides.

The two empty bikes sitting next to ours were like a punch in the gut. A haunting hint at what was to come. How many more empty rides would I have to see? How many bodies would pile up in this war?

'You can't save everyone, my love.'

"No," I said and kicked my bike into gear, "I just condemn them."

Chapter 21

NAOMI

Chase left to go God knows where. According to Tanner, he had business to attend to. Guess he couldn't have been too concerned about me.

Whatever, I didn't need him. I was perfectly capable of taking care of myself, like now. I was cleaning up his crap hole apartment. There wasn't much in here to clean but still. Someone should dust the place. I could practically see it in the air.

There were more interesting things to do. I was helping that bitchy girl, Jaz, make drinks before Tanner locked me back up in here.

He claimed an emergency came up, and he couldn't watch me anymore. I didn't need a babysitter, but I didn't want to be confined in here either.

My thoughts started to run wild thinking about all the stuff Tanner had said. How Chase lost his family and that crap about love. The longer I thought about it, the more it made sense.

That house was like a shrine. Nothing had changed in years. Chase didn't even pick up the unbuilt swing set in the back. How much did you have to care about someone to not be able to go back to the place you called home? If that wasn't love, I didn't know what was?

Which was the exact reason I decided to clean. The day I agreed with Tanner was the day I'd officially lost my mind.

I closed the drawer, swept my hands together and looked around. This place looked pretty good. Almost livable. Almost.

The tweed couch had to go along with that scratchy blanket. Thankfully I found a replacement in the closet. If I had to spend one more night with that thing abrading my skin, I was going to have to book some serious time at the spa. A complexion like mine took maintenance.

Speaking of which.

I grimaced at my nails. It was definitely time for a manicure. The color was starting to grow out. Since I didn't do the acrylic or gel–why mess with perfection–I could technically do it myself. But come on, who painted their own nails nowadays?

My brow lifted when something crashed against the other side of the door.

"Oh shit," *Tanner?* "Come on, man, don't do this shit to me."

I heard the jingle of what I thought might be keys, followed by Chase's voice.

"Put it in the lock," another thump on the door, "it's right there."

"I's trying."

My brow further arched when Tanner giggled. Yes, giggled. Like a little school girl.

"I had it the wrong way."

Chase burst out laughing, and I was assuming by the loud thump, fell over. Great the idiots were home, and they were drunk.

The doorknob jiggled, moving the door enough to rattle a picture of a Harley hanging on the wall. I just cleaned that. If those two morons broke the glass, I was going to kill them both.

I stopped and tipped my chin. Was I becoming my nanny?

The door flew open as two dumbasses spilled into the room.

Tanner and Chase hit the floor with an oomph and then lifted their wobbly heads up at me.

"Whoa," Tanner's eyes crossed for a second. "How come I see two of her?"

"I wish there were two of her," Chase tried and failed to pick himself off the floor.

I rolled my eyes. "You couldn't handle two of me."

"I'd sure like to try, though."

A big smile spread across Chase's face, and I was awe-struck for a second. This was the first time I'd seen happiness reach his eyes. The way they sparkled lit up his whole face. *Just like they did in that picture.*

I shook my head, snapping out of it, and huffed out a sigh. Lucky for them, I spent a lot of time at parties and was used to dealing with drunk idiots. Bed was typically the best remedy. More than a few times, I'd helped Logan fall into his.

"Alright." I walked over to Chase.

Him I'd help, but only because I had to share a room with him. Tanner... I glanced over at the other man who was struggling to close the door as he crawled out into the hall. He was on his own.

"Come on," I said, holding my hand out.

He took it, but instead of getting up off the floor, he pulled me down on it.

"Chase, " I argued while struggling to get back up, "stop it."

I was not a floor girl.

In a fraction of a second, he twisted his arm around my waist and pulled me on his lap. Holding me tightly against him. "You're so pretty."

"Yes, yes, I know. I'm gorgeous, now can we get on the bed?"

The corner of his mouth lifted in a sly smirk.

Oh for the love of...

"Not for that."

Even I had to admit it was cute when he popped his bottom lip out in a pout.

"Puppy dog eyes don't work on me, mister." Though his kind of were. . .

His hand snaked around to my ass, making me squeal as he slapped his palm down and grabbed a firm handful.

"I know something that works on you." Next thing I knew, his nose was buried in my neck and a deep growl vibrated from his chest. "You smell so fucking good."

It took every ounce of willpower I had to suppress a shiver when his tongue slithered across my skin.

"Chase…"

"Yeah, Baby, say my name." His other hand wrapped around the back of my neck and twisted my head to give him better access. "I wanna hear you fucking scream that shit."

Why did it have to feel so good to be manhandled by him?

Okay, we were getting sidetracked here.

Unfortunately, he wasn't letting me go. Chase continued to molest me, pawing at my body as his mouth worked a hot trail up the side of my neck. That I didn't mind. Nor did my pussy. I don't think I'd ever been this wet.

If he wasn't drunk, I might've considered letting him fuck me. My problem came when I tried to shift away. His strong hold on me tightened to the point that it hurt to move. He wasn't going to let me go. So, I decided to try a different approach.

"Baby, I don't want our first time to be like this," I purred, and slipped my hand under his shirt.

He was so much firmer than I thought. All hard and powerful. What would it feel like to have his naked body on top of mine. *Focus Naomi!*

"I want you to be sober, so you remember what it looks like when you make me come all over your cock."

Huh? I actually did want that?

Chase stiffened and flopped his head back. "You're not making me want to stop here."

The mischievously innocent glint in his gaze made me for just a second reconsider.

"How about I make you a deal? You get up on that bed," I nodded at the mattress, "and I'll let you fondle my boobs all night."

His eyes fell down to my breasts. "Shirt off?"

Sure, why not.

"Shirt off," I agreed.

Like a kid in a candy store that couldn't wait to get his treat, Chase released me and let me help him get up off the ground. Bastard was heavy.

It took a lot more effort than it should've to move him a few feet. By the time I dropped him on the bed, I was out of breath.

And my work didn't end there. He was far too inebriated to undress himself. As tempted as I was to let him sleep in his clothes, I had to sleep beside him.

Demin fabric wasn't comfortable for anyone to rub against all night. Besides, he'd seen me naked. It was only fair he returned the favor.

That was a mistake.

Once I'd stripped his clothes off, and he was lying there in nothing but a pair of black boxer briefs, I couldn't stop staring. The man was utter perfection.

Smooth, tanned skin stretched over the dips and curves of hard muscle. His tattoos only added to the attractiveness of his phsyique. Tanner's words came back to me as my eyes landed on the names inked in Chase's flesh.

'There's only one thing that makes this shit life worth living.'

"Come on, Princess, we had a deal." Chase folded his arms behind his head and smirked up at me. "I want that shirt off."

I rolled my eyes and pulled the fabric over my head. A deal was a deal. There was enough time for me to drop my shirt on the floor before Chase grabbed my wrist, pulling me down on the bed beside him.

One arm draped around my waist, tucking my back into his front, while his hand immediately began palming my breast.

He seemed content like that. Gently squeezing my tender flesh as he nestled in. I had to admit it was nice, lying there in his arms with his body warming up mine. I liked it. It made me feel calm and safe. I'd never felt that before.

Mind you I'd never cuddled before or been the drunken object of someone's desire—not like I was for Chase anyway—I was just something for them to do. And when we were done, I left. No one asked me to stay. No one wanted me to stay. No one clung to me like he was now.

"Chase, can I ask you something?"

"Hum?" he grunted into my neck.

"Do you believe in love?"

Chase braced his forearm on the bed and propped himself up to look down at me. "Why?"

"I don't know?" I shrugged and shifted my gaze away. "Just curious, I guess."

"You know, don't you? About Sam?"

I nodded. There was no point in lying.

He sighed and fell back on the bed. "Who told you?"

"I found the house."

It was quiet for a few minutes, and then…

"Is the swing-set still in the back?"

If a heart could physically break from a few words, then those were the ones that would do it.

"Yeah."

Why did I say anything? We were having a nice night–well, nice for us–and I had to go and ruin it by asking a stupid question.

I was about to apologize when his arm came back around my waist. Only this time, his hand didn't go for my breast. It tugged on the waistband of my pants.

"What are you doing?" I shrieked and shot up.

Chase pushed me back down and held me to the bed with a hand around my neck.

"Calm down, Princess," he growled in my ear, "I'm not gonna fuck you. I just want a taste."

"That was not the deal!"

In an instant, everything changed. Chase went from playful to full-on feral. He ripped my pants off my flailing legs and rolled on top of me.

"I don't give a fuck what the deal was. You're my captive. I can do whatever the hell I want with you," he barked down at me. "Or did you forget, Daddy doesn't care? You're just a girl."

"Fuck you, Chase." I snarled back at him.

The rage burned brightly in his eyes as his lips curled in a tsk.

"I told you, Princess," he flipped me over before I could slap him. "You have to earn my dick."

His fingers dug into my hips, pulling me up on my knees as I twisted around and swung my arm back. I got him, just barely.

My nails scraped across his arm, drawing fine little lines of red. He answered my assault with one of his own. By smacking his palm down on my ass, so hard I jolted up the bed. The worse part, my ass wasn't the only thing burning.

"Don't you…" I stopped mid-threat and smashed my face in the bed.

Chase shoved his fingers in my pussy and hit that damned spot.

"Look at that sweet little cunt." He pulled his hand out, gave my clit a firm slap, and slid his fingers back inside me. "Dripping with need. She knows who her master is."

"Fuck you," I moaned into the blanket.

"Keep tempting me, Princess, and I just might." His other palm slid across my ass and up to my back hole. "Except I won't take your pussy."

The threat was clear and not something I was afraid of.

"Go ahead," I groaned back at him while fisting the blanket to fight the pleasure he forced out of me.

"Hate me all you want." Two more pumps of his fingers, and I was going off. Screaming my ecstasy in the bed.

"I'm the only man who can make you come," he leaned over, flattening his chest on my back, and growled in my ear. "Like it or not, Baby, your pussy is mine."

Chapter 22

CHASE

Not sure where Naomi was when I woke up. I knew she was still in the clubhouse somewhere, none of the guys would let her leave, but she wasn't in bed beside me. She had to have left after I fell asleep.

I wasn't letting her go when I was awake. I didn't like the idea of her sleeping somewhere else, which in itself bothered me.

What I did to her last night shouldn't have happened. I might've felt bad about it if I hadn't walked downstairs after my shower and met her scowl. Her snarky tone rang through my ears like nails on a chalkboard.

"Have a good sleep?"

My brow arched. Fuck that. It was about time someone put her in her place.

"Because I sure didn't."

"Funny," I sauntered over to the bar where Jaz had set out break-fast. "You seemed pretty relaxed after you came all over my hand."

Tanner snickered in the corner and then quickly stuffed a forkful of eggs in his mouth. Though neither said anything, the smirk on Beast and Snake's lips told me they were amused as well.

"You molested me," Naomi shrieked with a foot stomp.

It was cute how her nose crinkled up in anger. So I shot her a smile, dropped down in one of the stools, and popped a piece of bacon in my mouth. "You liked it."

"You listen to me, Chase Mathers," she stormed over and wagged her finger in my face. "The next time you come home all drunk and gropey, I'll knee you in the nuts."

I swept her hand away and snickered, "Yeah, cause that worked real well for you last time."

Beast opened his mouth to say something, but Jaz shook her head. I snorted. Pussy. Letting his woman call the shots. Who was the man in that relationship? Last I checked, Jaz didn't have a pair of balls hanging between her legs. Not that I'd fucked her or anything.

When you grow up together, you see shit. One thing I should've learned from childhood was how girls teamed up, which I was kindly reminded of when Naomi's hand swung through the air.

The bacon went flying from my mouth as my face twisted to the side. I stopped long enough to glare at Beast, who just shrugged in response.

Tanner, of course, was buckled over, clutching his stomach in laughter. Snake was the only one that didn't seem to care either way. He sat at his table and continued to eat as if nothing was going on.

"How's that work for you. . ."

I was up and out of the chair before Naomi could finish speaking.

"Don't push me, Princess. I have one hell of a headache." That headache being her.

She didn't back down, puffed her chest out, and stepped right up to me, brushing those perfect tits against my chest. "Good. I hope it hurts. You are such a..."

Fuck, it was a turn-on to see her like this. Pretty face twisted in a snarl while the rest of her screamed femininity. Her golden hair cascaded down her back, sweeping off the soft curves of her hip with each snide little tip of her head.

This girl was the epitome of the metaphorical wild mare that needed to be broken, and my lasso was hard and ready to go. I'd bend her over and fuck her right here if there weren't other people in the room.

My eyes fell down to her pouty pink lips, wildly flailing insults. All I could see was how they looked wrapped around my cock.

Naomi snapped her fingers in my face. "Are you listening to me?"

"Nope."

I'm not sure if it was blatant honesty that set her off or the fact that Snake choked on his food and coughed out, "Damn."

Either way, she was really pissed now, waving her hand back and forth while snarling out more insults.

Fuck it.

I grabbed the back of her head and slammed my lips down on hers. She fought at first, mumbling protests in my mouth. And like the wild mare she was, all it took to reign her in was one hard tug on the back of her head.

She was putty in my hands after that, melting into my form while swirling her tongue around mine. Let me just say, Jaz's world-famous breakfast didn't have shit on her.

"I told you, Princess," I pulled away from her and stared down at her swollen mouth, "I own your pussy." I tugged her closer and softly growled in her ear, "Now, calm the fuck down, or I'll fuck you right here in front of everybody."

"You wouldn't?"

I arched a brow. "Try me."

A chime rang out overhead, causing all of us to look around for the source. When I didn't see anything, I started to think it was someone's phone—Tanner was always fucking with people's ringtones—until it went off again.

"What the fuck is that?" I muttered.

Jaz was the one who answered, "It's the doorbell."

"We have a doorbell?" Tanner perked up and glanced at Jaz with a cocked brow. "How long have we had a doorbell?"

"The more important question is," Snake's face curled in a grimace, "Who the fuck puts a doorbell on a clubhouse?"

That was a good question.

"The doorbell has always been there," Jaz shook her head and sighed. "Idiots."

The chime went off again.

Naomi cocked her hip. "Is anyone going to get that?"

Beast, Tanner, Snake, and I all looked at each other, unsure. Did we want to know who it was?

"Oh, for fuck sakes," Naomi hissed and sauntered out the door.

I did the only thing any red-blooded male would do. I pulled Naomi back into the room and waved the guys over, where we all took out our guns and slowly made our way down the stairs. Because who the fuck rings the doorbell at a clubhouse?

I put my hand on the doorknob, nodded at the other guys to make sure they were ready, and swung the door open. And who did we see standing outside with a pleasant smile on her face? Ava, that's who.

It wasn't some crazed man with a machete that gave us a heart attack. It was a five-foot fuck-all blonde with a big red bow in her hair.

"Is Naomi here?" She sang like she was asking her dad if Naomi could come out and play.

"I could've shot you," I growled.

"Why?" She quickly glanced behind her, "Was I supposed to bring something?"

Was she supposed to bring something? I just... what the hell... I can't...

I sighed and waved her past, "Naomi's upstairs."

She gave a little nod, said, "Thank you," and skipped inside.

Something caught my eye, causing me to stop her before she climbed the first step.

"Is that blood?"

"Oh yeah," Ava looked over her shoulder at the big red stain on the back of her shirt. "Those guys really shouldn't have tried to grab me."

Tanner straightened up from his spot behind the banister. "What guys?"

"I don't know they had these patch things on their vest. Hey," she pointed at one of the patches on Snake's cut, "kind of like that. I like the color of yours better. Red is so overdone."

We all stopped and looked at each other. Reapers.

"Where did they grab you?"

"The van's out there," Ava lifted her arm and pointed out at the road, "but don't get too excited, they don't have any cookies. Liars."

With that, she skipped up the stairs.

When I stepped outside to investigate, the first thing I saw was a pillar of black smoke rising in the air. The closer we got to the chain-link fence, the more unnerving the scene became.

About a block down the road sat the van or what was left of the van. All we found was the charred burnt-out frame of what used to be a van. Pieces of the vehicle were everywhere, sticking in trees and laying across the roadway.

"What the fuck?" Snake muttered.

What the fuck indeed? I lifted my gaze to half a tire hooked on the top of the fence and then scanned the road. Even more disturbing was the lack of bodies.

We found one of the Reaper's cuts soaked in blood, but that was it. No fingers, or feet, or any sign that people were there. One little girl did this? There was no fucking way.

I wanted to chalk this up to Wilder, but I told him to keep an eye on the house, and that's exactly what he'd do. Fucker was probably perched on one of the rooftops staring at it through a scope right now. Which wasn't exactly a comforting thought. But this?

Tanner picked up a piece of metal and tipped it in the sun. The faint remains of words were still visible. Free cookies. "I love this girl."

Snake and I cocked a brow at each other. Tanner was into some risky shit, but Ava Whitley gave new meaning to the term risky. That girl was just as likely to cut his nuts off as she was to suck his dick.

Fuck, I wouldn't be surprised if she ate the fucking thing. Soon enough, we wouldn't be calling him Playboy anymore, we'd be calling him Dickless.

"Seriously," he reiterated by pointing at both of us, "all you fuckers stay away from her."

He had absolutely no worry about that from me.

Snake didn't say anything. He just spun around and marched back to the clubhouse.

"Where are you going?" Tanner called after him.

"To get the girl some damn cookies."

Chapter 23

NAOMI

While Ava leaned over the table and easily clacked two balls in the pockets, I wonder how the hell I'm supposed to hit anything anywhere with this thin ass stick?

Why was I even playing this game? Oh right, because Ava showed up at the place I was being held captive like she was here for a friggin playdate. I was really trying hard to remember why I loved her.

"Oh, I forgot to tell you," Ava lined up her next shot, "there's a rumor going around campus that you're pregnant."

"What?!"

I wasn't the only one shocked. Chase choked and spat out his beer. Spraying it all over the floor, I just helped Jaz clean. Well, clean may have been a strong word. I assisted by pointing out spots she missed.

She was not very appreciative of my assistance, told me to do it myself if I thought I could do a better job. I knew I could do a better job, but she wasn't going to get any better if I did her work for her.

"P-pregnant?" Chase's wide eyes met mine, and I was tempted to slap some sense into him.

"Oh, calm down, Romeo. I have to earn your dick remember." I rolled my eyes. Pfft, earn. "So unless you have super pussy seeking sperm, I think we're safe."

Not to mention I was on birth control, which I stayed on top of, got my shot right before I came to school—not taking any chances in that department.

Relief visibly washed over him as he settled back in his chair.
Moron.

I swear guys lost their mind at the mention of the word baby, except for Parker. He was happy when he found out he knocked up Lana.

Considering she was only seventeen, I highly doubted she felt the same way. They were making it work, though. Weston and Winslow were kind of cute, and Ava loved those babies.

All she ever wanted was to be a mother, and Ryker took that away from her because she decided to stand up for me.

So yeah, Ava may be a little unhinged and murderous at times, but I'd never abandon her. She gave up the one thing she wanted most for me, and I'd give up my life for her.
Speaking of babies...

I turned my attention back to Ava. "Why are people saying I'm pregnant?"

"I don't know. A few people asked where you were, so I told them you were dealing with 'personal issues.'"

My face dropped as her fingers hooked doing quotes in the air. "Did you do the air quotes when you said personal issues?"

"Well, yeah."

I let out a sigh and dropped my face in my palm. *She's your best friend, you can't kill her.*

I could beat her with this stupid thin stick, though.

"The whole campus has been weird lately."

She bent over. and I couldn't help but notice Tanner in a chair behind her. His elbows were on his knees, chin in his hand, and a lovestruck look on his face as he watched my friend. That poor, dumb, fool.

It was just him, Ava, Chase, and I in here. That big guy left with Claire and the other one, Snape, or Snarl or whatever, threw a bag of Oreos at Ava and left. A bag she refused to share, by the way.

Maybe it had something to do with the blood on her shirt. I didn't ask. Blood on Ava wasn't new. I did make her change. Seemed like the thing to do since I had a bag of her clothes with me. Still pissed at her for that.

"Cammie said someone tried to grab her. Some other girl claimed guys on bikes threatened her, and Bailey is convinced she's being followed. Said something about a hill moving or shifting," Ava waved her hand dismissively. "I don't know. I think she got a bad batch of acid or something."

"Is that so?" I swear to God, if Chase and his cronies were threatening my girls. . .

"Crazy, right? I told campus security that we didn't know anyone with bikes."

My face dropped again. Seriously?

"Um, Ava, these guys have bikes."

"Really?" She stood up and looked at Tanner and Chase with big sparkling eyes. "Like those tandem bikes, cause those things are really cool?"

"No." Only Ava would think when someone said they were threatened by a couple of guys on bikes that they were on tandem bikes. "Motorbikes. Like Harleys and stuff."

"Oh," she frowned and waved her hand. "I don't think she was talking about those. Now tandem bikes, those things are memorable."

Wednesday was hazing. Apparently, Friday was tandem bikes.

Tanner tipped his head to get a better view of her ass, I was assuming, and muttered, "I'm definitely going to get one of those."

"Really?" Ava lit right up. "Will you let me ride it?"

"I'll let you ride anything you want to."

"Okay, it's a date then," she sang happily and then focused on her next shot.

Tanner straightened up and looked around with wide-shocked eyes before getting out of his chair.

"Where are you going?" Chase quietly growled as Tanner walked past him.

"To get a motherfucking tandem bike."

Chase rolled his eyes up at him, giving Tanner a look I didn't like. "A couple of guys on bikes? Don't you think we have bigger things to worry about?"

Tanner threw his head back and groaned, "Fine."

I narrowed my gaze on Chase's knuckles, tightening around the bottle in his hand. I know Ava was dismissing all the girls' claims, but Chase seemed pretty upset for it to be just a bunch of rumors.

So, I sauntered to him, reached over his shoulder to grab my glass of water, and whispered, "Stay away from my sorority."

Nobody fucked with my girls.

"It's not me," he hissed through clenched teeth.

I was briefly distracted by his phone vibrating on the table. I knew the name displayed, Riley, but it was the twenty-three missed calls that made me lift a brow. Why would Chase be ignoring Riley?

I thought they were super tight. Even more suspicious was the way he scooped his phone off the table when he saw me looking at it.

Whatever, if he wanted to ignore Riley, that was his choice. I'd ignore her too. Besides, that wasn't the issue here.

"I swear to God if one of those girls gets hurt because you decided to interject yourself in my life..."

"I got it, Princess."

"Do you?" I challenged with a cocked hip.

His hard glare met mine before he snatched his beer off the table and stormed away.

Tanner tipped his chin at Chase as if asking what's up with him. I shrugged and returned to Ava. Not my problem if he didn't like what I had to say.

We finished our game which Ava won, and then sat down for a little girl talk, or what I thought would be girl talk. Instead, I ended up listening to Ava go on and on about the various places one could ride a tandem bike.

When she got an idea in her head, it was next to impossible to get it out. A half-hour later and she had a whole European trip planned. Riding past Buckingham Palace on a bike built for two was not my idea of fun. I'd never been happier to get someone a drink than I was when Ava frowned at her empty glass.

Perfect excuse, I thought and scooped up the cup to go in the back and get her more wine. Why a bunch of bikers had wine, I didn't know. Didn't really care. Though I did have to say, this place wasn't as bad as I thought it was.

It was kind of like a bar. There was a backroom fully stocked with alcohol and snacks and a kitchen, which Claire seemed to be in charge of. I might even be starting to kind tolerate the place. Except for the shag carpet, of course.

My ears perked up when I walked in the back and heard a quiet voice.

"It's the only way."

Chase?

I snuck over to the shelf and peeked around the corner. Chase was pacing in the back by a couple of kegs. There was a look on his face I hadn't see before.

His brows were knit together as if he was arguing with someone, but his eyes had this fierce glint in them, almost like determination.

"Of course I can."

I half expected to hear someone answer him, and when I didn't, I lifted up on my tiptoes to see if he was wearing a Bluetooth or something. That was when I realized there was no one there. Chase was talking to himself.

"No," he barked out. "Stop it, Sam. He's always been my responsibility."

My hand flew to my mouth, muffling my gasp as my heart fell in the pit of my stomach. He wasn't talking to himself. It was worse. He was talking to her.

I wanted to cry for him. Run up there and wrap my arms around him and say everything would be okay, but I couldn't promise that. As long as he held onto a memory, he'd never be okay.

"Chase," I whispered and stepped out from behind the shelf.

His back instantly stiffened.

"Are you alright?"

He was so not alright.

He spun around and forced a smile on his face. "I'm fine."

I knew something about forced smiles. We couldn't appear to be the perfect family without looking happy.

"Are you sure, because…"

He stepped up and pressed his fingers to my lips.

"Shh, it's okay. I know what I have to do."

Why did that sound ominous? "Do you?"

There was that smile again.

"You go have fun with your friend." Chase cupped my face and leaned in to kiss my forehead. "Everything's going to be alright."

When someone says everything will be alright, it wouldn't. Just like I'm fine meant anything but. I didn't get a chance to say anything, though, because Chase walked out of the room before I could.

A sinking feeling grew in my gut as I watched him leave, and I briefly wondered if I should go after him, but Tanner strolled into the room, giving me another option. I mean, he knew Chase better, right?

"Does Chase often talk to himself?"

Tanner braced his elbow on one of the boxes and cocked his head at me. "What do you mean?"

"Well, I came in here, and he was saying it's the only way and talking about responsibility…"

Tanner made the distance between us before I could blink and was tightly gripping my shoulders.

"This is important, Princess," the look on Tanner's face was officially freaking me the fuck out. "What exactly did Chase say?"

"He said it was the only way. That it was his responsibility," I explained. "Then he told me he knew what he had to do."

Tanner spun around, kicked a box, and yelled, "Fuck."

"What's going on?" I demanded.

"You remember when I talked about people spiraling."

I nodded. "Yeah.

"Chase just hit bottom," Tanner said and ran out the door.

Chapter 24

CHASE

I sat on my bike, looking down the hill at the Reaper's compound. It looked like ours for the most part—same type of buildings and layout. Jax didn't even have enough imagination to design his own compound. There was one difference, though.

My eyes narrowed on the extravagant three-story house in the center. That was where my brother was. How did I know this? I grew up listening to him talk about how one day, he'd own a house with green shutters and a Kalamazoo Gaucho grill which I so happened to be staring at right now.

There weren't many guys walking around. I counted four, maybe five, that I'd have to get through. Most were probably still asleep. Jax liked to party. He probably had half the club up all night. I could make it, might get shot on the way, but that was okay. I didn't plan on walking away.

Flipping open my saddlebag, I checked on the brick of C4 I had stashed inside.

'Don't do this, Chase.'

"I have to." I sighed and looked back to the compound. "It's the only way to stop him."

'No, it's not. The club needs you.'

Two of my men died in that raid, and now those girls were in danger. No one needed me. I was a curse on this earth. A curse I planned on curing with one last ride.

'What about Naomi?'

That name caused my brows to pull together. I couldn't shake our last meeting. The way she was staring at me, with worry shining in her green eyes. It'd been a long time since someone had looked at me like that. But Naomi was strong, she'd be okay.

'Is she? You heard what her father said.'

"She's fine."

At least she seemed fine. She didn't look broken-up, or say anything about it. Then again, knowing Naomi, she wouldn't. Besides, there was nothing proving she even heard what her old man said.

'Of course, she did.' Sam scoffed in the back of my head. *'Don't be another person in her life that hurts her.'*

I grumbled out a groan and dropped my forehead on the handle-bars of my hog. "What do you expect me to do, Sam?"

'Let me go.'

I sat back on my bike and stared up at the sky. This was the kind of day Sam loved. She'd wake me up all excited with a picnic breakfast ready to go. I used to look forward to those moments when it was just her and me and a clear blue sky. Now, I dreaded seeing that cloudless perfection.

'It's okay to be happy. Move on with your life.'

It was the same plea I'd heard countless times over the years. Just like all the other times, I gave the same answer.

"I can't."

Before Sam could say anything else, I revved my hog and kicked it into gear. Before I could start my descent, Tanner rolled up, skidding to a stop in front of me.

"What the fuck are you doing?"

The purple flames painted on the back of his sled tugged at something in my chest. Riley put those on there. Tanner asked her to do it, not because she was family but because she was damn talented. And she took that shit seriously, spent weeks perfecting the hues and shades.

I could still see her face all scrunched up. If every thirteen-year-old concentrated that hard, school would be a breeze. She was bound and determined to do her best because she didn't want to let Tanner down.

'And now you're letting her down.'

"Do you really think I'm going to let you do this?"

My brow cocked at Tanner's firm eyes. Let? No one let me do shit.

"Get out of my way, Playboy." Twisting the gas, I revved in warning. I'd drive right through him if I had to.

A voice called out from behind me. "Not gonna happen."

Fuck.

I rolled my eyes back to Beast, who was parked behind me with his arms crossed.

"Beast? Really?"

"Yeah, fucking Beast." Tanner barked back at me, "You're lucky I didn't drag Mannix's ass out that hospital bed."

He wouldn't have to drag shit. If Mannix knew what I was planning, he'd ride here with a broken back and one arm to stop me.

"This is the only way." Jax had to be stopped at all costs. They had to know that. Besides… "I can't have any more bodies on my hands."

"Bullshit!" Beast growled. "Those bodies aren't on your hands. They're on your brother's."

My point exactly. How many more people would Jax kill just to get at me. I didn't ask for this. I didn't want the power our old man gave me, but I took it because I thought it was the right thing to do. Honor his wishes. Look what that got me.

"What am I supposed to tell Riley?" Tanner asked, "Sorry, Chase decided to go kamikaze."

"Works for me."

"Great, let the girl lose someone else she loves."

That was a low blow. Riley lost her mom last year in a car accident. Derek and I decided not to tell her that her mother was drunk at the time. She'd been through enough of that shit growing up.

Neither one of us wanted her to know alcohol won. The girl already blamed herself for her mother's addiction, thought if she was a better daughter, things would've been different.

'How's she going to feel if you do this?'

Tanner must've sensed my hesitation because he said sighed and said, "Come on, let's get you home, your woman's waiting."

Your woman's waiting. I liked the sound of that.

What if she ends up like Sam?

An image of Naomi staring up at me with dead eyes flashed across my mind, causing my hands to tighten around the handlebars. Mannix was already in the hospital. Who would be next? Tanner? Beast? Jaz? One ride down a hill, and I could save Naomi. I could save them all.

"Fuck this." Beast's growl was the last thing I heard before something hit the back of my head, and everything went dark.

When I came to, we were pulling into the clubhouse. Beast had me strapped to the back of his hog with my face pressed against his back. Which was about ten feet closer than I wanted to be to the fucker.

Tanner nodded at me as we pulled to a stop. "He's awake."

"Good," Beast grumbled and stepped off his hog, "I can slap him around."

I scrubbed a hand down my face and rubbed away the ache in the back of my head.

"You guys didn't stop anything. I'm just going to go back out there."

"Uh-huh." Tanner folded his arms across his chest, "How are you gonna do that without a bike, genius?"

What did he mean? I looked around, scouring the yard for my hog, but I didn't see it anywhere. We always brought our brothers' rides back. It was sacrilege to leave it behind.

"You left it?"

"Nope." Beast unhooked the rope strapping me to his ride, "We blew it up."

What?!

I sprang up, going chest to chest with Beast. "You fucking blew it up?!"

Tanner nodded. "Sure did."

I didn't know who I was going to kill first. The big fucker giving me the smug smirk, or Tanner. Either way, they were both gonna die.

"He seems pretty pissed," Beast leaned to look over my shoulder at Tanner. "Funny for a guy that claims to not care about shit."

"Yeah, Chase, what's the big deal?" Tanner cocked a brow my way, "You were gonna blow it up anyway."

"A guy who has nothing to live for shouldn't care about a bike," Beast pointed out.

I let out a relieved sigh. They did all this to prove a point. So I might not kill them, just fuck them up a bit.

"Ha, ha, very funny. You proved your point," I held out my hand. "Now, give me my keys."

"Oh no," Beast shook his head, "we blew that shit up."

My eyes went wide as I glanced from Beast to Tanner, who nodded and mimicked an explosion with his hands.

"It was beautiful," he said, "there were pieces everywhere. You should've seen it."

My jaw dropped. They were kidding, right? Somebody tell me they were fucking with me.

"Sorry, brother," Beast slapped a hand down on my shoulder, "you've been grounded until further notice."

With that, they left, leaving me to stand there searching for my bike, which I didn't see anywhere. Not even a trace that they'd had it brought back.

They actually fucking did it. I couldn't believe it. I was definitely going to kill them now. I looked at the door to the clubhouse.

And I had just the fucking gun to do it with.

I charged inside and stormed up the steps, taking two at a time. If the goal was to make me forget about my plan, then they succeeded. I didn't feel any of the determination or urgency I did before.

There was just rage, burning a hot trail through my veins. So much so that I didn't stop to open my apartment door. I lifted my foot and kicked it in.

'Calm down, Chase. They were only protecting you.'

"Protecting my ass," I growled at Sam and threw open my top dresser drawer, where I normally kept my 9mm.

It wasn't there.

"Where the fuck is it?"

'You would do the same.'

"No, I wouldn't."

I searched the rest of the dresser and still came up empty. Did someone clean up in here? Fuck. Maybe it was in the desk.

'You're really going to kill them over a bike?'

"I'm not gonna kill them." I began rifling through the desk, pulling open drawers and shuffling around papers. "Just shoot them a little."

They'd survive a leg shot.

'Don't you think you're overreacting?'

"Shut up, Sam." Never fuck with a man's ride.

"She's not here, Chase."

My back stiffened as I slowly turned to see Naomi standing in the bathroom doorway.

"She can't hear you," my jaw ticked, "Sam's gone."

"Fuck off, Princess," I growled and pulled open another drawer. "I'm busy."

Naomi crossed her arms and leaned against the doorframe. "If you're looking for your gun, I got rid of it."

And just like that, my wrath had a new target.

Chapter 25

NAOMI

Chase froze with his hand still in the open desk drawer and slowly rolled his glare my way. "You what?"

The darkness openly displayed on his face sent a shiver up my spine. I'd never seen him look this mad.

"I got rid of it," I repeated despite the warning bells going off in my thoughts.

After Tanner's reaction, I didn't think it was a good idea to have weapons around and based on how hard he was clenching his jaw, I'd say I was right.

"You don't need to be around guns right now."

"I don't need…" Chase roared, place his hands under the desk, and flipped it across the room.

I flinched as objects crashed around the room and again when the desk smashed into the wall, knocking three pictures off their hooks. I was wrong. Mad wasn't the right word for what was pulsing through Chase's large body, causing a vein in his forehead to throb.

"You don't get to decide what I need."

"I just thought…"

"Don't think, don't speak, don't do anything but get on your fucking knees when I tell you… You know what?" He tipped his head at me. I didn't like the look in his eyes. "That's a good fucking idea. Come here."

I lifted my chin and firmly stated, "No."

"Does it look like I'm asking?"

"Does it look like I care?" I shot back.

That was apparently the wrong thing to do. Chase was across the room, tearing me out of the bathroom before I could even think about closing the door.

"What do you not get, Princess?" He slammed me back against the wall, briefly knocking the air out of my lungs. "I tell you what to do, and you do it."

"Is that what Sam did?" I coughed out.

I watched a flash of guilt shift his expression before the rage deepened.

"You don't get to talk about her."

"Why not?" I snarled and shoved him back, "She's the one calling the shots, isn't she? I heard you talking to her."

Chase stepped back and ground out, "You don't know what you're talking about."

Oh, but I did. I knew all too well. Chase wasn't the only one who had ghosts haunting his thoughts.

"Does she answer you?" I asked, taking a step closer. "Do you hear her voice when you sit alone at night?"

"Shut up!"

"She's not here, Chase."

"SHUT UP!" He yelled louder.

But I didn't. I couldn't. As harsh as this was, he needed to hear it.

"She can't whisper sweet things in your ear…"

His hand shot out, wrapping around my neck as he slammed me back into the wall.

"Shut," he leaned in, hissing in my face, "the fuck, up."

"She's dead, Chase."

A growl so loud that it vibrated the wall erupted from his chest. He pushed his weight on my shoulders, causing my legs to buckle and forcing me down on my knees.

I landed hard and would've fallen over if he didn't have such a firm grip on my hair.

"Open your fucking mouth," he ordered while unbuckling his belt.

Unable to move my head, I rolled my eyes up and peeked at him through my lashes. "It's not gonna bring her back."

"I said," he pulled his hard and ready cock out and slapped me in the side of the face, "open your fucking mouth."

"Chase," was all I got out before he slammed himself down my throat.

It was all I could do not to moan as his taste exploded across my tongue, and he face-fucked me. I braced my palms on his thighs and took it, opened my throat and welcomed every bit of anger and hatred he thrust into me.

"See this? This is all your mouth is good for." His cock pulsed and throbbed, growing harder with each stroke. "To be my little cum dumpster."

He popped his dick out of my mouth and brushed the tip over my lips. "Come on, Princess, beg for your supper."

"Does it make you feel better to hurt me?" I tipped my chin up to look at him. "Or does it make her voice louder?"

Next thing I knew, I was being dragged across the floor by my hair and then flung on the bed. Chase was on me before I could balance myself, tearing the clothes off my body.

I didn't fight him. It wasn't the same this time. This wasn't a game we were trying to win. He needed this. He needed to let go.

"She's gone, Chase," I said as he tugged on my hips and pulled me up on all fours. "Doing this isn't going to fix that."

But it might fix him.

"You don't know when to fucking stop, do you?" The hard head of his cock lined up with my opening. "Guess I'll have to show you."

He shoved inside me in a strong thrust, stretching my pussy around his girth.

He groaned.

I moaned.

Then he fucked me.

Hard, rough strokes that touched all the right places. Igniting nerves, I didn't know I had. It felt so good and yet so sad because he still couldn't accept the cards fate had dealt him.

"Fuck," he ground out and dug his fingers into my hip, pulling me back to meet his thrusts. "Is this what you need to shut the fuck up?"

I moaned and arched my back, lifting my ass so he could go deeper. "Is this what you need to forget, Sam?"

"Stop," thrust, "saying," swivel, "her," thrust, "name." swivel.

I fisted the blanket, forced back the scream of ecstasy threatening to pour out of my mouth, and whispered, "Sam."

Chase growled so deeply I felt it in my core. Within one second, he had me flipped around with his hand on my neck as he slid back inside me.

He picked up the pace, using me hard. "Don't say her fucking name."

My pussy pulsed around him, hungry for his length, but it was the look on his face that had me entranced. He was fighting hard to hold onto his anger. Once that was gone...

"Sam."

I watched Chase's brows furrow as his fingers tightened around my neck, digging into my flesh.

"Stop it."

No, I wasn't going to stop.

"Sam," I wheezed out through my constricted windpipe.

He tried to ignore me, tried to concentrate on furiously pounding into my pussy. But I wasn't going to let him.

Every time I said her name, I saw him break a little more. If it took my last breath, I would pull him back from whatever ledge he was teetering on.

As Chase roared out his orgasm and slammed into me one last time, I reached up and cupped his cheek.

"Her name was Sam." Tears brimmed in his eyes as they met mine. "And she's gone. You need to let her go."

A tear slid from the corner of his eye, rolling down his face and splashing on my chest, filling me with the pain I could see in him.

"I can't."

"Yes, you can." I pulled him down, resting his forehead on mine, and whispered, "Let her go. Let them both go."

He broke, clutching me tightly as he collapsed and let it all out. I held onto him. Let him cry on top of me while I ran my fingers through his hair.

"It's okay." I kissed the top of his head and tightened my hold. "I'm not going anywhere."

Chapter 26

CHASE

I woke up the next morning feeling lighter than I had in years. The last time I could breathe this freely was the day before I lost them. My baby boy and my wife. Sam, my sweet, lovable ray of sunshine. I didn't think there'd be anything after her.

I rolled over and carefully swept the hair off Naomi's sleeping face. Naomi wasn't a ray of sunshine. I wouldn't be surprised if the sun avoided her, but she was stronger than anyone I'd ever met.

She managed to do what no one else could. Make me accept the truth. My whole world went up with that car, but for the first time, I started to think that maybe, I could build a new one.

Naomi's old man had no idea who his daughter was or what she was capable of. She was fierce and loyal and a little bit sweet. She let me brutalize her and then held me for hours afterward.

There was no ridicule or snide remarks when I broke down, only tender strokes and reassuring words. Naomi Prescott wasn't just a girl. She was the girl.

I propped myself up on my elbow and traced the lines of her pretty face. Someone up there decided to send me an angel. She may not be the harp playing, kind cherub people expected, but she was the angel I needed.

"Are you watching me sleep?" Naomi's green eyes fluttered open as a snarl curled her lip. "Ugh, creep."

I couldn't help but snicker. "I guess I am being a creep."

I couldn't stop staring at her. Memorizing the way her pouty lips tightened in a sneer as her nose crinkled. It was cute.

"What's wrong with you?"

"Nothing's wrong with me." *I'm just seeing you for the first time.* Her tanned skin had the most beautiful glow.

"Why are you acting weird?"

My hand swept down her neck and over the swell of her breasts, tugging the blanket as I went. "I'm not acting weird."

"Yes, you are, and stop looking at me like that," she slapped my hand away. "It's freaking me out."

I rolled my eyes and fell back on the bed. "Can't you just let me enjoy the moment?"

"What moment? There was no moment."

"There was." *Until you woke up.*

"You listen to me, Chase Mathers..."

I stared up at the ceiling, praying whoever sent me this angel would take her back.

"Just because I let you fuck me last night doesn't mean you can molest me in my sleep..."

Alright, that's it.

I shot up, pushed Naomi back on the bed, and crawled over her.

"Trust me, Princess, when I fuck you, you'll be wide awake," I lifted myself enough to rip the blanket out from between us and forced my knee between her thighs, "and begging me for more."

Her hands flattened on my chest, giving 'em a shove. Too bad for her. I wasn't going anywhere. Especially not since I knew how much she wanted it. Her hot little pussy was pressed up against my knee, creaming all over my skin.

"If you think what happened last night is going to happen again…"

Oh, it was happening again. If I had anything to say about it, it would happen again, and again, and again.

"You've got another thing…"

I shut her up by pressing my fingers to her clit and giving a firm pinch. My mouth curled in a smirk when she sucked back a gasp. One thing I'd learned about my snotty princess, she liked a little pain with her pleasure.

"I'm sorry," I teased while slipping my fingers in her tight channel to milk her g-spot. Two pumps, and she was moaning like a cat in heat. "I didn't quite hear."

Her back arched off the bed as she groaned out, "God, you're an asshole."

"An asshole whose fingers you're about to come all over."

Naomi's sharp glare snapped up to mine, and that's as far as she got. I hooked my fingers and gave it my all. Not stopping until she had to clutch onto my shoulders to stop the world from spinning.

It was so fucking hot watching her come apart under me. I could smell how wet she was. Feel the headiness of her arousal in the air. I wonder what she tasted like.

Let's find out.

Before she had time to catch her breath, I crawled down her seductive body and threw her leg over my shoulder. If she said anything, I didn't hear it.

The only thing my mind could focus on was the sweet honey coating my tongue as I licked her from entrance to clit, and back down again. That's it. I was fucked. This woman was mine, and god help the fucker that tried to tell me otherwise.

I felt her fingers burrow in my hair and growled against the tug she gave. Because I wasn't going anywhere. Fuck that. This pussy was mine to do with what I wanted, and right now, I was one hungry motherfucker.

Did I hear her scream? Fuck yeah, I did. Did I feel her nails digging into my back? Yup. Could I tell she'd had too much? I sure could. But did I care? Fuck no. I devoured that hot little cunt until Naomi was a panting mess.

And I didn't stop there.

I pulled my head away from her legs and moved up to her face, where I dragged my tongue over her cheek and down to the shell of her ear.

"Hang on, Princess," I breathed while lining my cock up, "Daddy's just getting started."

Why daddy? I don't fucking know? But I'd wanted to say that shit to her since she walked in my tattoo parlor.

Her mouth parted, lips forming words that were lost the instant I thrust inside her.

I groaned long and loud as her walls squeezed around me, shooting heat up my shaft and into my balls. "So fucking good."

This girl haunted my dreams for almost a year. I'd jerked off to her image so many times my dick hurt, and when I finally let myself have her, I was too pissed to enjoy it.

I wasn't pissed now, though. I was hard and ready to go. Grunting as her pussy fluttered around me as I pumped inside her.

"Chase," she moaned.

"No." I shot up, wrapped my hand around her delicate neck, and hooked her leg over my arm. "Call me Mr. Mathers."

The first time she said that shit, I damn near came, and fuck me if she didn't do it again. Peeking up at me all seductive through her lashes while breathing out, "Mr. Mathers."

There was no holding back then. I rode her hard and fast. When she didn't give me what I wanted, I flipped her onto her stomach and drove into her from behind. She squealed and bucked back, telling me I was at the right angle to hit the spot I wanted, which I did. Again and again and again.

When her pussy clamped down, spraying her orgasm all over my cock, I grabbed onto her ass and pulled those firm cheeks apart, so I could watch my dick slide inside her.

Seeing my cock dripping with her cum gave me an idea.

I flipped us over, so I was on my back with her on top of me.

"Come on, Baby," I growled, giving her ass a firm smack, "ride that cock."

"You can't tell me what to do," Naomi twisted her neck, glaring over her shoulder at me. "I'm not one of your submissive sluts."

My brow arched.

Oh, she wanted to play this game, did she?

Naomi didn't know that Tanner told me he'd caught her watching something on my laptop. There were only three videos on there, and they all had the same theme.

I was all for equality. Let women be women and all that shit, but in the bedroom, I was king. If the princess didn't want to submit, I had no problem making her.

"You seem to forget, Princess," I grabbed her hips and slammed her down on me, "My cock's the only one that can make you come."

Which was exactly what I was after. Naomi was a squirter, and I wanted to see that shit spray all over my chest.

"You think that makes you king?" she snarled.

I responded with another hard slap to her ass. "You're damn right it does."

"You're such a..."

I smacked her again.

"Mysoganistic..."

And again.

"Prick."

And again, only this time, she had to brace her hands on my thighs to stay upright.

"Keep it up, Princess and this ass will be red in no time."

I gave her one last slap and groaned at the red handprints on her creamy flesh. She liked it too. Her pussy clenched every time I hit her.

The shit I wasn't prepared for was when she fell into it and started riding me. Bouncing her ass off my stomach as she pumped her pussy along my shaft.

I wasn't fucking her anymore.

She was fucking me, and god damn if it wasn't one of the hottest things I'd ever seen. I thrust my hips, matching her movements, and watched in euphoric glory as the sexiest women alive rode me like a champ.

When Naomi's nails dug into my skin, and her body shook, I couldn't stop it anymore. Seeing her slick drip out and coat my skin had my balls tightening.

I grabbed her hips and slammed her down hard, reveling in the way her inner walls tightly milked me.

"Jesus, fuck." I snarled and pumped into her furiously until my heart stopped with an orgasm so intense my fingers were digging into her hipbones.

I FLIPPED the desk onto its legs and grumbled out a string of curses. Naomi kicked me out of the bathroom. Might've had something to do with the fact that I fucked her in the shower and again when we were drying off.

When I went for round four, she kicked me out. Now she was in there, having another shower and washing my scent off her. That, I was not happy about.

I wanted her to walk in a room smelling like she was just fucked so other assholes would stay away from her. Now, I'd have to mark her all over again. What a shame that was. The corner of my mouth lifted.

Once I had the desk back in place, I began collecting all the other crap that got flung around the room. My laptop was a lost cause. The smashed pieces of what remained of it were scattered everywhere, along with books, files, and other papers.

That temper tantrum was going to cost me some organizing time. I glanced over at the bathroom door as the shower shut off.

It was worth it.

Who'd have thought that losing my shit would be the best thing to happen to me? Hours ago, I was ready to ride into my death. Things weren't completely better.

I still wanted to kill my brother, and my imminent demise was in the back of my mind, but there was also a little hope. There was something I had to come home to now, and maybe that would be enough?

"What the hell happened in here?"

My back stiffened.

Riley?

No. It couldn't be. She was at home in Ashen Springs.

My face dropped when I turned around because my niece wasn't at home where it was safe. She was standing in my doorway, all five-foot-two of her—glaring at me with those deep blue eyes.

"Riley? Why are you here?"

She flipped her black hair over the Minnie Mouse hoodie she was wearing and crossed her arms. "Um, maybe because someone wouldn't answer their phone."

Yeah. Should've known that was gonna bite me in the ass.

"I was busy."

"Doing what?"

Planning my suicide.

"I had things to deal with," I explained while dropping the pile of papers in my hand on the desk. "In case you forgot, I'm trying to run a club."

"Bullshit," she shot back at me.

I loved how full of piss and vinegar my niece was, but I didn't take her shit when she was a kid, and I wasn't taking it now.

I crossed my arms and glared right back at her. "I know everything seems perfect up there in la, la land, but the rest of us have real adult shit to deal with. I can't drop what I'm doing every time you call, besides you should be more concerned with school. And who the hell let you drive to Miami anyways. Does your dad know you're here?"

Fucking Derek. That guy needed a slap.

"Oh no," Riley swung her hand through the air, "don't you turn this around on me. I wasn't the one ignoring someone's phone calls."

This again?

"I wasn't ignoring your…"

"Tanner called me."

I stopped mid-sentence. *Well, shit.*

"What did he say?" Could she hear the guilt in my tone? Because I could sure feel it tugging at my heart.

"He said enough." Riley's face softened as she released a sigh, "He's worried about you, Chase. We're all worried…"

She stopped talking when the bathroom sink turned on and rolled her gaze to the closed door.

Fuck.

"Who's in there?

I shook my head. "Nobody."

"Nobody?" She cocked her hip out and tipped a brow at me. "So who turned on the water then?"

I stood there trying to figure out what to say as the running water rang through the room like a doomsday clock. Until this moment, I hadn't really considered Naomi's age.

Pretty sure Riley wouldn't like knowing I was fucking a girl a year older than her. I really was that skeezy uncle I warned her about.

Riley stared at me.

I stared at her.

Then the bathroom door opened, and Naomi sauntered out.

"Chase, you're out of shampoo, and the stuff you've been using is so bad for your hair. You should really buy shampoo from a salon."

Riley's jaw dropped. "You've got to be kidding me."

Chapter 27

NAOMI

My lip automatically curled when I lifted my chin. Ugh, she was here.

"No, I'm not kidding you. You should never use store products on your hair." I rolled my gaze down the black locks slung over Riley's shoulder. "That includes Pine-Sol."

"As opposed to the buckets and buckets of cum you use," she shot back.

"I don't know what you and Micha do, honey, but I prefer to clean myself after a man fucks me," I waved at the towel on my head. "Hence the wet hair."

That's right, I knew Chase was her uncle. Just like I knew my comment would piss her off. And oh boy, did it. Riley's face got all red as she stomped her foot.

"Really?" She snarled at Chase while holding her hands out to me, "Her?"

"Ah?" Chase shifted his gaze between Riley and I, "I mean…"

I sighed and swung my hand through the air. "Relax, it's just sex, it's not that big a deal."

"Like fuck," Chase roared, shocking us both. "I swear, Naomi if you touch another guy, I'll break his damn neck."

My brow rose while my heart fluttered. "You're not going to start that mine crap now, are you?"

"Yeah, I'm gonna start that mine crap." His angry glare locked with mine." You got a fucking problem with that?"

Did I have a problem with it? I'd seen other guys get all possessive and never really put much thought into it.

"That depends," I said, "do I get to do the same thing to you?"

Chase's expression morphed from anger to smug satisfaction. "You wanna claim me. Baby?"

"Oh my god," Riley groaned.

I don't know what her problem was. The man was clearly hot. All power and perfection as his shoulders gracefully rolled back and he stalked towards me. Maybe that was the issue?

Maybe Riley wanted him. For some reason, that pissed me off. I literally had to stop my hands from fisting.

I straightened my back and walked up to Chase, and dragged my finger down his chest. Riley Adams could have Micha Kessler. She wasn't getting my man.

"I reserve the right to knock out any woman who eyeballs you." I shot Riley a look so she'd get my meaning.

She rolled her eyes in response.

Chase's hand wrapped around the back of my neck as he pulled me into him. I went with it, pressing my body up against his and moaning a bit when his mouth grazed my ear.

"And then what?"

"Then," I trailed my finger down his arm, pausing to admire the firmness of his muscle, "I want you to fuck me in front of her."

"You're about to get fucked right now," he growled.

"Oh my god." Riley threw her hands up in the air. "Have I landed in some weird alternate dimension? Some one has to be playing a prank on me."

Chase sighed and pushed off the desk to take a few steps away from me. I was tempted to follow, but I'd made my point.

"Look, Riley, Naomi is…" He stopped and looked back at me for a second before continuing, "Well, she's Naomi."

Gee thanks.

"And like it or not, we're together now. So I expect you to treat her with some respect."

That's right.

I smiled brightly at Riley's shocked expression.

Until Chase added, "And I expect you to do the same."

I crossed my arms. Why should I respect her? What did Riley Adams have to offer? Besides a sharp attitude and a smart mouth?

"You can't be serious?" Riley cried out.

Finally, we agreed on something.

"I mean… look at her."

Look at me? Look at her? What the hell was she wearing? The emo look was definitely a trend, but that didn't include digging through your childhood closet.

"Cute shirt." I tugged the towel loose and ran my fingers through my hair. "I had one just like it when I was five."

Chase shot me a dirty look, and Riley's face dropped.

"No," she said, shaking her head. "This is not happening."

Chase scrubbed a hand down his face. "Riley…"

"No," she repeated. "I'm not doing it."

"Sorry, honey," I sang, "It's done."

Riley's face tightened. She looked at me, glared at Chase, and then stormed out.

"Shit," Chase muttered and followed.

I stood in the room listening to their footsteps before eventually sighing and heading out the door.

Guess we're following the crybaby now.

Chapter 23

CHASE

Riley's hair flew behind her as she ran down the stairs at record speed. How did someone so small move so fast? Part of me thought I should just let her go. Riley was just mad.

Eventually, she'd come around, but a bigger part thought, what if she doesn't? I couldn't lose the last piece of Sam I had left. Don't get me wrong, Naomi was growing on me, but I loved Riley. I couldn't let her leave like this.

"Riley, stop," I called out as she tore through the lounge.

Tanner tipped his chin in her direction. "What's going on?"

"Naomi," was all I had to say.

He nodded and muttered, "Oh yeah, good luck with that."

As tempted as I was to beat the fucker, I continued chasing my niece.

I didn't catch up until she burst out the front door and stopped dead in her tracks. Standing just outside, leaning against his Jeep, was Micha.

"Tell me something, Mouse." He tipped his head, looking over his sunglasses at Riley, "What the fuck are you doing in Miami?"

Wait... she didn't tell Micha she was coming? That wasn't like Riley. As much as I hated it, I knew she loved that boy, listened to her whine about how much she'd miss him when he went to college, and he wasn't her first stop. What the fuck did Tanner say to her?

"Micha?" Shack flashed across her face, which Riley quickly came back from. Rolling her shoulders back and hardening her expression. "I don't have to tell you everything I do."

"Like fuck you don't!" He barked back at her.

Every fiber of my being screamed at me to knock the prick out. I got where he was coming from, though. If I was pissed as hell that she drove down here, then I could just imagine what Micha was feeling.

There was a war brewing, which had already spilled onto his campus once. Neither one of us wanted her anywhere near this city. And since clearly, she wasn't listening to me...

"I didn't think you'd mind."

Even I cocked a brow at that one. I had to hand it to Micha, though. He was a lot calmer than I was.

"Let me get this straight," he pushed off his Jeep and took a few steps closer to her. "You thought you could drive into the middle of an MC club in Miami, and I wouldn't give a shit?"

Riley rolled her eyes. "Well, when you put it that way."

Micha took off his sunglasses, blew out a breath, and brushed a hand down his face.

"I blame this on you, by the way," he said while looking at me.

"What the fuck did I do?"

"If you'd have answered her calls, she wouldn't be here now."

Couldn't really argue that.

As if to reiterate my thought, Riley crossed her arms and huffed out, "He's right."

How did this go from them arguing to a gang up on me?

"At least then I wouldn't have had to see you with her."

"Naomi?" Micha asked.

Riley swung her eyes his way. "You knew about that?"

"I suspected." He shrugged.

Son of a bitch! Did this motherfucker plan this shit? Is that why he brought me all that info on Naomi's old man. I knew that shit was too easy. All that shit he was spewing about standing up for their own. I thought for sure he was trying to pull me into his society crap. His old man sure was.

"You want to tell her why Naomi's here?" I cocked a brow at Micha. "Or should I?"

"What's he talking about?"

Micha glared at me, making me snicker when his jaw ticked. Go ahead, little boy, try me.

In an instant, things changed. Micha's face went from challenging to curious as he twisted his neck to look at the road behind us. That's when I heard it. The quiet rumbled of bikes in the distance.

Not something out of the ordinary, especially around here. That's not what froze my heart dead in my chest.

ACDC's 'Back in Black' mingled in the air with the sound of roaring engines. Only one person I knew played that, and it was never for a good reason.

Panicked, I went for Riley, but Micha was faster. He grabbed her, curling his body around hers as a stream of bikes rode by, reigning a hail of gunfire on the compound. Naomi chose that moment to step out of the clubhouse.

All I could think as bullets sliced through the air was, not again. I bolted, dodging the rides parked around us and jumping over obstacles to grab her and throw her down on the ground, covering her frail body with mine.

Naomi screamed and tucked herself into me, but all I could hear was the unnatural growl rumbling by.

The compound came alive, men ran out, yelling and returning fire. I stayed where I was, protecting my girl from the onslaught of my brother's wrath. Bullets whizzed by, cutting into buildings, tinking off metal, and cutting into the ground around us.

Tanner came bursting out, jumped over my curled-up form, and kicked a bike over to give me some cover.

I yelled one word at him, "Riley."

He took off, scouring the chaos for my niece.

The bike helped some, but not enough. As I lay there, coving Naomi, three rounds burrowed into my flesh. At least I thought it was three.

The first one hit me in the side, burning a path of fire across my gut. The next got me in the thigh, and the last the shoulder. Couldn't really feel anything after that. My whole body went numb. I could barely hear Naomi's voice.

"Oh my God, Chase."

"Stay down," I told her and pressed her further into the ground.

I could take the agony and pain. What I couldn't take was losing her. Not again…

"Can you say, Daddy? Daa-dee."

I snickered and shook my head. "Babe, he's only six months old."

"Six months tomorrow," Sam pointed out.

I sat back and watched as my wife bounced Maddox on her knee. His face lit up, and he laughed, filling my heart with joy.

"Who's a big boy?" Sam sang to him.

This right here, this was what life was all about. A beautiful wife and perfect baby, a man, couldn't ask for anything more, which was exactly why I planned this trip. I'd been so busy trying to handle things since my old man passed, I'd been neglecting my family. A nice quiet day at the lake was just what the doctor ordered.

"You want some chocolate?"

Sam rolled her blue eyes. "Duh?"

"Okay, fair enough." I laughed.

She'd live on the stuff if I let her.

"How about you, little man? You want some chocolate too?" I held my hand out, and Maddox quickly grabbed my finger, wrapping his tiny little digits around mine. "I'll take that as a yes."

I stepped out of the car and strolled into the store. It wasn't a big place and kind of in the middle of nowhere, but everything I needed was here. Including Carl, who was waiting for a drop-off. Nothing wrong with doing a five-minute transaction during family day.

After giving Carl his kilo and collecting my money, I loaded up on choco-late and walked back out. The sun was shining down, lighting up Sam's face as she turned Maddox to look at me and raised his little arm.

"Wave to Daddy."

"CHASE! Chase! Oh my god, wake up."

My eyes fluttered open, revealing the blue sky overhead. Was it over? Was that why I was on the ground? Where was Naomi? I wanted to call out her name, but nothing came out when I opened my mouth. I couldn't move either. Pain rocketed up my spine every time I tried. I needed to know that she was okay.

"Oh, thank God." Naomi's sparkling green eyes appeared above me as her palm brushed against my cheek. "Hang on. The ambulance is on the way. You guys are going to be okay."

Why was she so worried, and what did she mean by you guys?

I rolled my head along the ground the same time Riley's screams pierced my ears. She was curled over Micha with tears streaming down her face while she screamed at him to wake up. But he didn't even flinch, just laid there limp as the pool of blood beneath him seeped into the ground.

He wasn't the only one bleeding. A deep crimson puddle soaked into the leg of Riley's jeans. She was hit. My niece came here to check on me because I couldn't take the time to send her a text, and she got shot.

Jax's voice rang out in the back of my head.

'You're gonna get them killed.'

He was right. I wasn't a curse. I was the finality. The tortured misery that brought only pain and suffering. Riley would be better off without me.

They all would.

Epilogue

NAOMI

I gently brushed the hair off Chase's face and dabbed the cloth on his forehead. It'd been almost forty-eight hours since the day my heart stopped. I'd never known fear like that. I was terrified laying under him, and not for me, for him.

People were shooting at us, and the stupid idiot was out in the open. He got shot three times for me. I couldn't stop thinking about that. Chase Mathers risked his life to keep me safe. Maybe love did exist after all.

Micha did the same for Riley and almost died doing it. He was okay now, but it was touch and go there for a while. Twice, he coded on the operating table.

Riley was a mess. Mr. Kessler's presence didn't help. He'd walked around the halls, demanding to be let in the room with his son. The hospital staff had to calm him down more than once. I'd never seen him like that.

It probably would've been worse if Micha's brother Mason came. I guess he was on a class trip, and their father couldn't get a hold of him. He was going to lose his shit when he found out. Logan was halfway across the country at MIT, but he was on his way. That wasn't important right now.

All I cared about was Chase. His wounds weren't fatal. He was out of surgery in a couple of hours. It was his mood that had me worried. He slept most of the time, which was to be expected. When he was awake, it was like he wasn't there. He'd stared blankly ahead and gave one-word responses, even to Riley.

He was not okay and probably cold.

Riley wheeled herself in and nodded at Chase asleep in the bed. "How's he doing?"

"He's cold." I tugged on the hospital blanket, trying to cover him up more. "Why do they make these things so thin? Who the hell could stay warm in this?"

"I'm sure he's fine."

"He's not fine," I snarled while raising my finger at the nurse carrying in a tray. "What is that?"

She glanced down at the cargo she was carrying. "It's his dinner."

"Get it out of here," I waved at her to leave, "he's not eating that."

"Ma'am…"

Did she just ma'am me?

"He has to eat."

"Not that! I'll get him some real food." I'll get him a damn blanket too.

"Naomi."

"What?!" I barked out at Riley.

She reared back in her chair with wide eyes and then turned to look at the nurse. "You heard the woman, get that shit out of here."

Apparently, the nurse didn't want to take on both of us because she gave me a snide glare and strutted out of the room with her tray in hand. I returned to my sleeping man and continued to dab the beads of sweat off his brow.

"You really care about him, huh?"

I rolled my eyes. Why was she still here?

"Listen, Naomi," Riley sighed, "Chase has been through a lot."

She thought I didn't know that?

"Just don't hurt him, okay? If you do, I'll have to hurt you, and he'll be all mad. It's not a good situation. Anyway," she turned her chair and wheeled away, "I'll leave you alone now."

"Riley."

She stopped and looked back at me, "Yeah."

"The same goes for Micha."

Don't get me wrong, I wasn't Micha Kessler's biggest fan, but I grew up with the guy. He was like family.

She nodded and left.

I stayed there for a while, watching Chase sleep until it was time to go order his food. There was this great little place that had the best steak, and most men I knew loved a good steak.

Since I didn't have my phone cause someone kidnapped me and my apparent best friend kept forgetting it, I had to leave the room to make the call.

On my way back, I ran into Ava, who was talking to Logan and his girl Shelby. Shelby was dancing around from one foot to the other while Logan and Ava stood there casually chatting.

"Oh my god," Shelby whined, "I need to see Rye, like now."

"Calm down, Baby. She was just shot."

That was the wrong response for Logan to give. Moron was all that flashed through my mind as Shelby's hand swung in the air, whacking off the back of his head.

"Logan Hudson, if you don't take me to see my best friend right now, you'll die of blue balls."

She may as well have torn out Logan's heart right then and there. His face dropped, and he quickly scurried her down the hall without even saying goodbye to Ava.

Rude.

I shook my head and stepped up next to my best friend.

"You know," Ava said, "I like that girl more and more every time I meet her."

As much as I hated to admit it, Shelby Grace was growing on me too. "She's alright."

Suddenly the hall was filled with squeals so loud I had to cover my ears. Riley came out of her room, and both she and Shelby screamed.

"Hey," I yelled as they ran into each other's arms, "keep it down. Chase is trying to sleep."

Ava leaned over and whispered, "I get that they're friends, but do they have to be all handsy like that?"

I grunted in agreement. There was such a thing as too close.

"Did you bring that blanket I asked for?"

Ava nodded and passed me a large plastic bag. One look inside made me want to shake my head.

"Ava?"

"Yeah?"

"This blanket has Care Bears on it."

"I know," Her big eyes turned my way. "Cute, right?"

I weighed the complications of trying to explain to her why a man like Chase would not want cartoon characters on his blanket and then decided it wasn't worth the headache. It would be easier to tell Chase that Ava brought it.

"Well, I'm going to go give this," I held up the bag, "to Chase. I don't suppose you brought my phone?"

Her nose crinkled. "Don't you have it?"

"No," I sighed, "I don't have it."

"You should never leave home without your phone. What if an emergency happened?"

I just stared at her.

"Geez, Naomi, think ahead."

"I'll remember that," I said while reminding myself that there were far too many witnesses around to commit murder. "I'm gonna go." Before I didn't care about the witnesses.

"Okay," Ava waved and skipped down the hall.

The first thing I noticed when I entered Chase's room was the empty bed. The second thing was the open bathroom door. Where the hell was he?

I dropped the bag and searched around. The wheelchair was still there, so I didn't think a nurse came and took him, and his clothes weren't in the closet.

It wasn't until I sat down on the bed that I noticed the folded-up piece of paper. Inside were written two words: *I'm sorry.*

Tanner sauntered through the door as I glanced up from the note. "Where's Chase?"

"He's gone."

"What do you mean he's gone?"

"I mean, he left," I slapped the note on his chest and headed out the door.

Tanner tipped his head and called out, "Where are you going?"

"I'm going to hunt his ass down."

You're not running again, Chase Mathers.

Not on my watch.

I would like to thank my beta readers, editor and work wives who helped me get through a rough time to bring this book out. And to my readers, I really tried hard to make this book a standalone, but I just couldn't fix Chase in one book. He is so much more broken then I thought, and no matter where the characters take me, I will follow. Naomi and Chase will get their happy ending in Frenemies. When that will come out, I don't know yet. I have Accident-Prone and the sequel to Innocence to write first. I should have a tentative release date for you soon.

Thank for reading Adversaires

If you enjoyed this book please consider leaving a review. Reviews are always much appreciated by authors.

If you'd like to be among the first to know about new releases and get an inside look into my world join my Facebook group T.L. Hodel's Murder Of Ravens.

Look for more books in The Order Of Ravens and Wolves.

T.L. Hodel is a Canadian author, poet and artist. Through coming up from a difficult childhood she excelled at writing, having her first poem published in junior high. When not writing she occupies herself with numerous crafts, hobbies and is an avid gamer and horror movie fan. She lives in Calgary with her kids and cat, (who is a complete asshat), and may have a slight weakness for true crime shows.

Connect with T.L. Hodel online:
www.facebook.com/groups/272402970612789/?ref=share
www.instagram.com/tarahodel
www.facebook.com/Author-TL-Hodel-102923044775313/

T.L. Hodel Books.

The Order of Ravens and Wolves:

Aftereffect

Scartissue

Happenstance

Accident Prone (coming soon)

The Lost Souls MC:

Adversaries

Frenemies (coming soon)

Deviant House:

Innocence

Innocence Defiled (coming soon)

Audiobook:

Aftereffect (being made by Just ask her productions)

www.ingramcontent.com/pod-product-compliance
Lightning Source LLC
Chambersburg PA
CBHW021309190726
48288CB00003B/766